Shot Across the River Styx

Samuel Jaye Tanner

Shot Across the River Styx © 2018 by Samuel Jaye Tanner.
All rights reserved.

Illustrations by Michael Swearingen

Happy Valley Improv LLC
PO BOX 354
State College, PA 16804

www.happyvalleyimprov.com

ISBN 978-1-97335531-0-0

Second Edition

DEDICATION

For Nick: I hope this book helps.

DISCLAIMER

This is a true story.

I disguised the names of Nick's parents. They've already been hurt so much, and I care about them deeply. And I changed the name of incidental characters so that nobody sues me.

The rest of the people in this book are real.

This includes the fictional character Magic 'Fucking' Johnson. Magic shouldn't be confused for a celebrity with a similar name.

And kids, please do try this at home. Making sense of an enormous, complicated universe is a good thing to do.

CONTENTS

- F R A M I N G   T H E -
S H O T

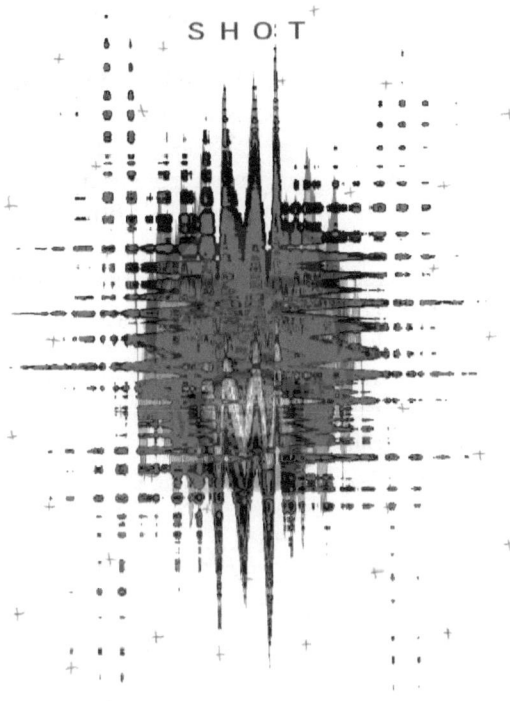

It has been ten years since my good friend Nick put a bullet in his brain. It has been two years since my stepfather, Jim, did the same thing.

Nick was one of the most intelligent people I have ever met. So was Jim.

Nick was so precise as he leveled up his characters in *Final Fantasy III*. Jim was a master carpenter, and could build seemingly anything. These were different intelligences. They were equally impressive to me.

One of the great things about people is how smart they can be.

Then both Nick and Jim put bullets in their brains.

One of the terrible things about people is how stupid they can be.

I don't know why Nick and Jim did what they did. Maybe if I were smarter, I would know. But I'm not. This is an enormous, complicated universe.

So I started to write.

***

This book about Nick and I began to take shape when I received a writing prompt in a class about teaching creative writing to high school students. I was pursuing my doctorate at the University of Minnesota when Jim put a bullet in his brains, you see.

The prompt was this.

Where were you last night?

After another in a series of reoccurring dreams where Nick had traveled back from the dead to visit with me, I responded to the prompt by responding to the dream.

Where was I last night?

Here's what I wrote.

I was asleep in my bed. Kinda sorta. I might also have been traveling. And in this maybe traveling, I swear you came to me, Nick. You were very much not dead.

We were at your parent's house. But we weren't

thirteen. And we weren't twenty-three. We were in our thirties. At least I was. There was a seriousness about you that wasn't there when you were thirteen. I suppose that is what a bullet to the brain does. It makes everything so serious.

So our conversation was heavy. I asked you how you had climbed out of your coffin. You explained that you hadn't really died.

We spoke. Something was missing. We couldn't quite connect. And then you were leaving again. I tried to tell you about your father. I tried to tell you about your mother. I tried to tell you about seeing them at my wedding. I wanted to tell you that it was as though they had died when you died. But you were fading out. And then you were gone.

In the morning, as I responded to a writing prompt, it occurred to me that I was sincerely curious. Where were you last night? Where was I?

I think that I was asleep in my bed. But who can be sure? And I figured you were a rotten heap of bones in a cemetery in Northeast Minneapolis. But who knows?

We were somewhere last night. I am certain of that much.

That is what I wrote.

And after I wrote, I packed up my laptop. Instead of putting a bullet in my brain, I went about my life as a high school teacher, a doctoral student, and a newlywed. Talk about busy. Talk about adult.

Nick, meanwhile, was a lump of decaying flesh in the ground.

On my way to teach high school that morning, I put Pearl Jam's *Ten* in the CD player. Nick and I use to listen to that album when we were thirteen. Nick's favorite song was the final track.

"Release me!" I sang along as my car barreled forward through an enormous, complicated universe. And I was surprised to realize that I was crying.

***

Here's a true story.

I first met Nick Wiseman when I was twelve. We became fast friends. And we stayed extremely close until, at twenty-two, Nick shot himself in the head with his dad's AR-15 assault rifle. He did this in his bedroom in the basement of his parent's suburban townhouse.

And then it was 2012 and I was thirty-two. Nick kept coming to me in my dreams.

I spoke at Nick's funeral. I was standing in front of a crowded room of mourners. The only thing I could think to say was this:

"I have so many stories I could tell you about Nick." I paused and, through my tears, my lips curled into a mischievous smile. I continued.

"None of them are appropriate for this occasion."

The crowd of people laughed at my joke.

While it didn't feel right to share Nick and I at his funeral, it does feel right to do so *here*.

So this book became a funeral ceremony. This is how I properly buried my friend Nick. This is how I released *us*.

- C H A P T E R 1 -

I was sitting in my classroom. It was six in the morning. I was thirty-two years old now. I'd been a high school English and drama teacher for nearly ten years. The students wouldn't arrive until seven. I had an hour of peace, an hour to write.

Times moves quickly, so I went to work.

A laptop was open in front of me. In fact, an empty word document glowed with potential. A story was coming. My mind was electrical energy. It felt like lightning was about to strike. There was a charge inside of me. Something had to happen, but I wasn't sure what.

My friend Nick had been gone for ten years. I was alone in my classroom.

I needed to write about Nick.

***

"Magic 'Fucking' Johnson," I wrote, "was a writer and a prophet, but mostly, he was a traveler. This was because Magic had been struck by lightning. Twice."

I looked up from the screen. The classroom was quiet. I was surprised. I sat down to write about my friend Nick. Instead, I was writing about Magic 'Fucking' Johnson?

Weird.

Shaking off my surprise, I continued to write. As I did so, I settled into Magic.

For now, I would need him.

***

"It was like getting electro-shock therapy from the universe," Magic wrote in the first chapter of *I Was Struck By Lightning Twice, So So Were You!*

Incidentally, this was the title of Magic's book about how he had been struck by lightning twice, returned from the dead, and learned how to travel through an enormous, complicated universe. It was something of a cult classic.

The self-help crowd ate it up.

Here's another excerpt from that chapter.

"The universe reached out to me, baby. Shocked me straight to the core. My kishkas were kishka'd. And it wasn't that low vault psychiatry-medicated-mumbo-jumbo stuff that don't leave no room for traveling. It was that delicious energy that shoots you right out of your head. Once you're ready to leave that head behind, the universe is the limit. By that, I mean there ain't no limits. It's clear skies and easy traveling, baby. All you gotta do is get shot out of your head and not worry you been shot out of your head.

Of course it hurt like hell, baby, but you need something to get you moving, get you traveling, get you living. Otherwise you're dying. And dying ain't no good. We need somebody to send us that lightning, baby, we can't do it on our own. That is what *they* are for.

They did it to me with a bolt of lightning, but it might hit you from somewhere else. It could be the sound of my voice. It could be the sound of *your* voice. Man, it could be a burst from an AR-15 assault rifle. But whatever it is, once that energy is conjured, there ain't no getting rid of it. Never. Once that energy starts singing, baby, it runs wild."

***

And I looked up from my laptop.

And I was confounded.

Magic 'Fucking' Johnson? Really?

I blinked. I chuckled. And then I started laughing. When we were twelve, Nick would have thought that my character's name was so stupid. Nick and I laughed at stupid things.

Where had Magic come from?

Sitting there in my classroom, surrounded by empty desks, I remembered driving by the cemetery where Nick was buried.

A few weeks before, I was coming home from another long day of teaching high school. Nick's grave was in a cemetery that was near my house in Northeast Minneapolis. Tired of singing along with Pearl Jam, I tuned into an interview on AM radio. It was a rerun of some talk show. The host was speaking with an author who had written a book. I wanted to be an author who wrote books. So I listened.

This author had been struck by lightning. He was pronounced legally dead. Then he woke up.

He claimed to have met twelve beings of inordinate light in the afterlife. Those beings had told him that everything would be okay. Everything. Then they sent him back from that space between spaces. And when he returned, he wanted to tell people that they had nothing to fear in death.

"They showed me it was okay," he kept saying to the radio host, "it would always be okay."

The radio host humored this lunatic.

The author's voice had this nasal, prepubescent quality. In fact, it reminded me of a note that had been conjured by a flute. Whenever he made mention of *them*, he emphasized the word as though he were using italics.

This author claimed to have been resurrected to share his message about death. So he wrote a book for people to read.

Listening to that interview, I thought about Nick. Where was he? Was he okay? What was he doing now?

Had Nick met *them*? Was he talking with Jesus? Was he roasting?

Who knows? I certainly didn't.

So many questions.

A couple of weeks after listening to that interview, Magic 'Fucking' Johnson emerged as I wrote about my friend Nick. Like the writer on the radio, Magic was an author who had been struck by lightning and returned to show *us* something. The difference? Magic got struck by lightning twice.

Weird.

By this point in my life, two people that I loved had made the choice to put a bullet in their brain. Suicide had struck me twice. It sent my mind racing, my fingers tapping away in front of a glowing laptop screen.

Okay.

Back in my classroom, I packed up my computer. I spent the day teaching high school. In the evening, I went to class at the University of Minnesota. Finally, I came home to my new wife, Katie.

"How was your day?" Katie asked after hugging me.

"Fine," I said. I was exhausted. I was working so hard. Such an adult. Nick wasn't working hard. He wasn't an adult either. Nick had been dead for ten years.

And I sprawled out on the couch next to my wife Katie. We watched South Park on Netflix until I became tired.

"I'm going to bed," I told her.

"Okay," she said.

We kissed, and I walked upstairs to our bedroom.

I fell asleep.

***

I was asleep but not really. Nick was dead but not really.

Talk about heavy.

We were interacting in a time and place that was entirely unintelligible. In fact, you could say that we were nowhere. Drifting. Boundaries were shifting in that space between spaces. There was nothing so ordered as weddings or funerals here, as books or interviews, as finality in life or death.

Nick and I were traveling.

Magic watched us with great interest. A lubricant to easy traveling, he could see that there was something very wrong with Nick and I. He wanted to play.

Magic tried to tell us as much. But we couldn't hear him. Not yet, anyway. We were two beings caught up in heavy stuff. Magic listened to us talk.

"You're dead," I told Nick.

"Nope," Nick said.

"What do you mean, nope? You shot yourself with your dad's assault rifle."

"I survived."

"You survived? I showed up that morning. All of us did. We sat in your parents' living room. Nobody said anything. Josh, Mike, and I sat there with your dad and mom for like eight hours. You were gone. Everybody was silent. We stared at the carpet. You were very, very dead."

Josh and Mike were two of Nick's closest friends during high school and into college. They were two of mine as well.

Nick shrugged his shoulders. He took a drag off of a cigarette and exhaled the most perfectly formed smoke ring you've ever seen.

Nick had been stealing cigarettes from his adoptive father Pete since he was twelve years old. He'd been stealing hid dad's mannerisms since Nick's American family flew to Korea to adopt him. Like his dad, Nick was fiercely stubborn, had a sharp intellect, and was precise when he fired an assault rifle.

Nick was so damned smart. When he decided to do something, he made sure to do it better than anybody else. Like playing *Final Fantasy III*. And blowing smoke rings. And putting bullets into his brain.

Nick was also so damned stupid.

I digress.

"I was at your funeral," I told Nick in that space between spaces, "I talked about you. I watched them lower you into the ground. You were in the coffin. You're dead."

"Whatever. You jackasses buried me alive. I climbed out, baby." Nick often added meaningless 'baby's' to the end of his sentences. The pitch of his voice would climb when he accentuated a sentence with 'baby.'

Nick also had a fondness for the term jackass. He thought everybody was a jackass. Especially me.

When I was twelve, he and I were messing around on the basketball court down the street from his house. I grabbed the ball from him. I screamed boom-shak-a-laka in honor of Shaquille O'Neal. Shaq screamed this when he broke the backboard with a dunk in a commercial from the early 90's. Nick and I thought that commerical was so stupid. So we laughed at it.

"Boom-shak-a-laka!" I howled.

Instead of executing a dunk like Shaq, I slammed the ball through my legs, and tried to bounce it off the backboard behind me. The ball came up and hit me in the groin. I fell to the ground in agony.

Nick laughed like a fool.

"Sam, you're such a jackass!"

When the pain wore off, I laughed with Nick. Both of us wore mischievous smiles.

Those playful smiles were often on our faces. Nick and I often did things we weren't supposed to do. Our teachers or Nick's mom routinely pointed this out to us. But we were rarely malevolent in our disobedience. We didn't mean to hurt anybody. So our smiles were mischievous, but harmless.

In this space between spaces, those smiles were hard to make out. So was Magic.

Was that dirt on Nick's face? Was that a smirk? Was there a hole in his head?

Nothing made sense here. Things were moving and shifting. Memories were forming as stories and then disappearing as quickly as they came. It was both the past and the present and the future. Everything was so confused.

But I felt an electrical charge. It was as though a storm were coming. Something was about to happen. Something was happening.

I looked at Nick, trying to see him.

"And so now you're back?"

I couldn't tell if Nick was trying to see me.

"I never left."

"Well okay, what've you been up to?"

"…"

"Okay."

"I gotta go."

"Go   where?"

"…"

Magic watched Nick and I disappear. He wanted to travel with us. A being of inordinate light, he wanted to teach us something. But we weren't ready yet.

***

And I woke up. And I drove to school.

I put my copy of Pearl Jam's *Ten* into my CD player. *Ten* was the first album I purchased.

I bought the cassette tape from Best Buy. And I let Nick borrow it when we were twelve. He couldn't get enough of it. Especially the song "Release Me." By thirteen, we knew every track on that album by heart. We'd play the tape on Nick's boombox as we sat in front of the television, playing Nintendo.

At thirty-two, I listened to the CD as I drove to work.

"I'll hold the pain," I sang at the top of my lungs, "release me!"

And I thought about Nick. I cried a little. It was ten years since he'd killed himself. I was well-adjusted, wasn't I? Where were these tears coming from?

I got to school, and I wrote. I conjured Nick. I made Magic.

And then students began arriving for school. My classrooms always burst with social activity in the morning. As the drama teacher, I've provided a home for countless students over the years.

One of my students came up to me.

"Mr. Tanner, what are you doing?" They asked.

"Writing a book about my friend Nick and the bullet he put in his brain," I smiled mischievously as I packed up my computer. What a dramatic thing to say to a high school student.

"Oh."

And I laughed at the absurdity of what I'd just told my student. And I taught high school. And then I drove home.

"I'll open up," I sang on the drive home, "release me!"

And then I went to sleep again.

Time moved quickly, you know?

That was my routine.

***

As I slept, Magic worked inside of me. And Magic responded to the same writing prompt that I'd responded to. I was his audience. Magic wrote it like this.

Where were you last night?

I'll tell you where you *was*, baby. You was unstuck, Sam. You wasn't sleeping. You wasn't awake. You came undone. Loosed into the universe. You was traveling.

Real traveling, Sam, sounds something like a basketball going through the net.

Woosh.

Don't laugh, baby. I'm serious. I'm talking bullet in your brain serious, baby. You came to a place between places and, in that place, you had an unutterable interaction with Nick. I know this 'cause I was there. I was there 'cause I was struck by lighting. Twice. And so now I'm anywhere and everywhere.

I'm anything and everything and everyone.

So so are you.

I want to help you say something, baby. I want to show

you how to make a storm.

We can put this thing right.

So I gotta teach you how to think with *this*. What's *this*? It ain't your head and it ain't your heart. I'll show you, baby, if you listen. And then *we* will fill the universe. Hell, we'll fill all of 'em.

You see, after I was struck by lightning the second time, thirteen years ago on this very day at this very moment, at this very second 'cause time don't mean shit, I was pronounced legally dead. But then, thirteen hours later, I came back from the dead.

How's that for taking a shot to the head? How's that for redirecting that shot back into the universe?

After I came back, I could do something. I could travel. In the middle of the night, when most people was stuck, I was doing some serious traveling. I learned to see with *this*, baby. That is the way that *they* see. That is how I saw *you*. And *you* are so wounded, Sam, and so is Nick. So I gotta teach *you* how to see the way that *we* can see Sam, if only *we* open *ourselves* up.

So in the middle of the day, when most people was stuck running this way or that, playin' their own careless and stupid version of basketball, I was laughing, baby. I could *travel* and I knew where all of *us* was going, where all of *us* had been, and what all of *us* was becoming.

Something set *you* loose, Sam, and so now I'm gonna teach *you* how to travel.

I tried to get your attention when you was talking to your friend Nick, but *you* was all caught up in some serious conversation. I couldn't quite make it out. It was all about assault rifles, coffins, and parents.

Talk about heavy.

Man, was I frustrated. There *you* were, two unstuck entities and all *you* could talk about was getting stuck again? I mean, put a bullet in my brain, will ya? How boring can ya get?

There was such life in *you*, Sam, and I wanted to let you

14

and Nick live. Nothing ever goes away. Once something is conjured, Sam, it can't disappear. *They* showed me that.

So I wooshed to the left and I wooshed to the right. I *am*Magic 'Fucking' Johnson, baby, so so are you!

I wanted to ask *you* if you had been struck by lightning too. Twice? Is that how *you* came unstuck? Is that how *you* started traveling?

Then both of *you*, so confused, vanished. Stuck again, baby. Probably getting up in the morning to kiss your wife on her cheek, to go to work, and to waste your time with all those silly ways that people waste their time. Games.

I was sad, baby, because I wanted to travel with *you*.

But there will be a next time. I see *you* now. I will come your way when *you* least expect it. I'll nudge ya a little bit. And next time *you* come unstuck, we gonna do some traveling baby. You seen the 87-88 Los Angeles Fucking Lakers, right? They ain't got nuthin' on what *they* got, baby.

We got some magic to do, Sam. *We* need something to be released.

Woosh, baby.

***

The alarm clock went off. I was exhausted. Once again, after showering and driving to work, it was six in the morning and I found myself sitting in a desk in my classroom. My laptop was glowing. I loosed myself into it. I came unstuck. I let Magic run wild.

"I just wanted to write about Nick," I wrote, "and now I'm writing about Magic Johnson?"

Twenty years after Nick and I watched the real Earvin "Magic" Johnson's announcement that he had HIV on TV, we were together again in a word document. It was so nice to be with Nick.

Nick had been like a brother to me when I was an adolescent.

Now, I was traveling back to him as a thirty-two year

old. Unlike Nick, I tried to survive in an enormous, complicated universe.

And I put my laptop away, surpised by Magic, and spent the day creating a storm in my high school classroom with my teaching.

That day, the storm in my classroom sounded something like this:

Woosh.

And then I went home, and fell asleep next to Katie.

***

It was three in the morning in Minneapolis. I was asleep, but not really. Nick was dead, but not really. Magic was traveling.

Really.

Magic sensed that Nick and I were caught up in another confused conversation. Like a note from a flute, Magic loosed himself into the universe. If you've ever watched Earvin 'Magic' Johnson the basketball player take his first step to drive the lane, you know something of what this looks like.

Nick and I were caught up in that space between spaces again. How long had we been tangled up in this unintelligible dialogue? Ten years? An eternity?

"Time don't mean nuthin', Sam," Magic called out from nowhere and everywhere at once.

I couldn't quite hear him yet.

Magic tried to get our attention. He did a cartwheel. Nothing. A summersault had the same result. Nothing. Magic recited the lyrics to Pearl Jam's, *Release Me*.

"I'll open up," he yelled with a nasal, prepubescent twang, "release me!"

Nick and I took no notice of Magic.

Magic blinked and conjured Nick's adoptive father, Pete Wiseman. Magic blinked again and conjured Nick's adoptive mother, Daphne Wiseman.

Pete was cleaning an AR-15 assault rifle dressed in hunting gear. Nick's mother was vacuuming the blank space.

Nick couldn't quite see them yet. And they couldn't quite see him.

But something was being conjured.

Magic blinked again and Pete was dressed in the suit that he wore to my wedding. Another blink and Daphne was wearing the black dress she wore at her son's funeral. Another blink and our friends Mike and Josh were standing around a hole in the ground. Another blink and they were gone.

Magic listened as Nick and I tried to connect.

"Nick, what're you doing here?"

"..."

"You aren't supposed to be here."

"Where else would I be?"

"Dead. Underground. I don't know."

"Well I'm not."

"What do you want to do?"

"Play video games?"

"Sure."

"..."

"Where are your parents?"

"I don't know."

"Where are we?"

"My house?"

"I don't know."

Magic almost burst with frustration. He screamed at us.

"I know where you guys are. You're traveling. And you don't even see it, baby. Listen to me. You guys are stuck and I can help. Nick? Sam? I know you, baby. I know you better than you know yourselves. *You* taught me something and now I gotta teach *you*. You just gotta let it come. Like good basketball, baby, you gotta let the game come to you now.

Just when Nick turned to notice Magic, I disappeared.

***

And I woke up.

And I drove to school.

And I sang Pearl Jam at the top of my lungs. Tears came to my eyes each time.

"Release me!"

And I got to school and I wrote.

And I recorded my dreams about Nick. These dreams felt like plays. I watched Nick and I as though I were an audience member.

And I wrote some more.

And I dreamed some more.

And then the cycle repeated itself.

What the hell was I doing?

Something was being conjured. It seemed as though whatever that something was, it was out of my hands.

***

And that is how this book happened.

I discovered that, the more I wrote about Magic, the more I wrote about Nick and Nick's suicide. Magic had lubricated me, as it were.

And it seemed the more I wrote, the more I wanted to talk about Nick.

"My friend put a bullet in his brain," was a hell of line. I started using it with my friends. I used it with students. I talked to anybody who would listen. And the more I talked about it, the more I wanted to write about what I was talking about.

Time moved quickly, and I found myself writing a weird book.

But it was as though I were writing a children's story. As much as I was trying to tell the story of Nick and I, I kept writing about a character named Magic 'Fucking'

Johnson.

Magic's middle name was important because it was so damned stupid. Juvenile. I was riffing on my first memory with Nick, watching Earvin Johnson admit he had AIDS. Magic was something that Nick and I might have dreamt up when we were twelve. He was a child's fantasy.

Magic wasn't married. He didn't teach high school, and he wasn't in graduate school. Magic didn't have to worry about being polite, about offending people. He could travel the infinite expanse of the cosmos with his mind. Magic could travel with his writing. He could heal the wounds of people who put bullets in their brains. He was not bound by limitations.

Magic was different than me.

Yes, Magic was weird. But I needed him. Magic was there to help me figure out the gaping hole that Nick had shot into his head.

Earvin 'Magic' Johnson had perfected his shot on the court. Magic 'Fucking' Johnson was helping me transform Nick's bullet from a tool of destruction into a beautifully endless basketball shot into the cosmos.

This book became the vehicle for that shot. It became a proper funeral ceremony.

During that conjuration, whether it was reminiscing with our friends Josh and Mike, talking with Katie, having dinner with Nick's parents, or talking to people about graduate school, stories about Nick just rolled off my tongue. I hadn't talked or even thought about Nick in years. But now he was here with me, he was alive.

I wrote a one-act that told the story of my reoccurring dreams about Nick. And I told stories to my high school classes about Nick's ghost visiting me in my dreams when I taught Hamlet.

It was weird. And it wasn't strategic. But that's how this book happened.

I came to think I was releasing Nick. This strange book was the only way I knew how to let him go. Something had to happen. And I had no idea how to make it happen. So I kept writing.

- C H A P T E R 2 -

Nick Wiseman was born in 1979, in Korea. Pete and Daphne Wiseman adopted him in the early 80's. They raised him in a townhouse in Arden Hills, Minnesota.

I remember Nick telling me that he didn't know when his real birthday was. Nick birth mother had left him in an orphanage in Seoul. This is where Daphne and Pete found him in the eighties.

Nick celebrated his birthday in July.

***

By 1992, Nick would get off at my bus stop so that we could play John Madden Football after school. Nick didn't have a Super Nintendo. I did. I'd put a frozen pizza in the oven. Nick stayed at my house until his parents made him come home for dinner. We were twelve years old. At least I was. Who knows how old Nick really was?

Nick and I played the original John Madden Football. In 1992, the Madden franchise hadn't cornered the market. This was before the graphics were any good, before the official NFL roster was licensed to the game, and before the game's release sparked an annual advertising campaign.

Nick and I first met because we rode the same bus home from Sioux Middle School. Sioux was nestled along the edges of North Oaks. A lavish golfing community, many of the students that attended Sioux came from North Oaks. Most of them were white. Most of them were rich. Most of them later attended Hill View High School with Nick and I. After high school, most of them had their college tuition paid for by their well-to-do parents.

Talk about copious amounts of wealth.

My father scammed his way into this upper-class neighborhood by purchasing a suburban paradise on the cheap from a high-school friend of his.

"It was a great deal!" Dad told me in a sardonic voice. "How can a Jew pass up a great deal?"

Dad moved my sister Christie and I three times in the

span of two years after he divorced Mom. He won sole custody of us because the judge ruled that my drunk mother was too unstable to raise two children. This was saying something, because my stoned father was pretty volatile himself. An insurance agent, Dad made an exorbitant commission and used the money as a down payment on that suburban palace. So we ended up in the affluent neighborhood of Arden Hills in 1990.

Nick's parents had a little townhouse buried within that antisceptic, suburban sprawl.

Nick was one of the few non-white students that went to Sioux. He was Korean. The running jokes about Nick through middle school and into high school involved his slanty eyes. After making those jokes, somebody would make the sound of a gong. Our friends would comment that Nick was the whitest Asian that they knew. He was certainly the whitest Asian that I knew.

I didn't know many Asians.

Nick and I got along immediately. He laughed at my jokes. I was new to the school district, I came from a single parent, Jew-for-Jesus-freak family, and Nick always seemed to *get it* when I made jokes about not fitting in.

Nick loved basketball. But he had shin splints. And he was short. And he was Asian.

I was chubby. And I was short. And I was Jewish. So I didn't care much for basketball.

But I was lonely. None of the normal, affluent white kids wanted much to do with me or my sarcastic edge. So when Nick asked me to shoot baskets with him at the court down the street from his house, I jumped at the opportunity. Nick had a mean three-point shot when he was twelve. I developed a pretty nice outside game of my own about fifteen years later. Nothing special. But I could keep up with the game.

This was because I didn't put a bullet in my brain. I kept trying to figure out what to do on the court. Nick did not.

We weren't good enough to play basketball for real, so we rented Tecmo Super Basketball from Mr. Movies. This was before NBA 2k whatever came out. Tecmo was the original sports series. Nick would sleepover at my house. We'd play video games all night. And we would do it again the next night. My dad would order us pizza. My sister Christie would smoke pot with her friends in her bedroom. Dad would smoke pot by himself in his bedroom.

"What are your dad and sister doing?" Nick asked me.

"Smoking pot," I told him.

"Oh."

In Tecmo Super Basketball, I always played as the Phoenix Suns. I would substitute Charles Barkley in at center. He scored sixty points a game. Barkley was so fast compared to the other centers. Even thought Barkley was fat.

"You love fatties because you're fat," Nick told me.

I laughed at him.

Nick thought it was cheating that I created the mismatch with Barkley. The computer controlled teams weren't complicated enough to counter the tactic. I told him it was good strategy. And when Barkley wasn't handling the ball, I'd kick it out to Dan Majerle to shoot three-pointer after three-pointer.

"Thunder Dan!" I'd shout as Majerle drained a shot from half court.

Nick used the Seattle Supersonics. Shawn Kemp gottwenty points and ten rebounds a game. Gary Payton got ten steals a game. Payton was Nick's favorite player.

"Look at those hands, baby," Nick gloated as Payton broke the record for steals in a game. "He's the glove, baby."

My nickname for Nick on the court was "the Glove." Like Payton, he had quick hands and could snag the ball from you before you knew what happened.

Nick's nickname for me was "fatty." Like Charles Barkley, I was fat.

Playing Tecmo Super Basketball with Nick was much better than playing Nintendo alone. I had somebody to make jokes with. Finally, I had somebody to laugh with me about my sister's stupidity, my father's neglect, or Bjork's newest music video.

"Is she dressed like a tree?" Nick said with laughter.

I chuckled with him. "I think so."

Another thing we laughed about was my father's strange habits.

"Why the hell didn't he have the light on?"

It was late on a Friday night, and Nick was raging.

We were upstairs in the loft. That was where Nick and I hung out and played video games during middle school. Dad and Christie were down the hall. By high school, I moved my bedroom into the unfinished basement, so I could stay up all night without bothering anybody. Nick did the same at his house. But in middle school, we hung out upstairs.

"I don't know," I told him.

"Who the hell takes a dump in the dark?"

"My dad?"

I was concentrating. Thunder Dan was eyeing up a 50-foot jump shot. The timing of my thumb needed to be perfect.

"He wasn't wearing a shirt," Nick said.

"That sounds like my dad."

"His back is so hairy."

"He *is* a Russian Jew."

Nick had gone downstairs to check on the pizza in the oven. On his way back up, he stopped in the bathroom on the main level. There he came upon my father. Dad was shirtless and sitting on the toilet in the dark.

"I feel unclean," Nick said.

"With good reason," I told him.

"That jackass," he laughed too.

So at thirteen, Nick and I laughed about stupid things. We made each other less lonely. Nick helped me cope with

25

the abnormality of my adolescence.

Yes, and for whatever reason, I vividly remember Nick and I watching a special press conference that Earvin 'Magic'Johnson's gave after he was diagnosed with HIV. Magic was giving some cheesy answers to a group of little kids about being tough and playing hard. But Magic had HIV. And nobody was asking any tough questions about dying, about how he contracted it, or about what his future would look like. So I turned to Nick and said, "Wouldn't it be funny if one of the little kids raised their hands and asked Magic what it was like to know that he was going to be dead soon?"

Nick and I howled with foolish laughter.

From then on, he and I were bound together on a certain trajectory. We had somewhere we needed to go, I guess.

***

When Nick wasn't spending the night at my house, I spent the night at his. Our routine was the same. We rented video games from Mr. Movies and played them all night. Oftentimes, we wouldn't go to sleep.

This was not a problem at my house. Dad was usually too stoned to care what we did. Our nocturnal habits were a problem at Nick's house. His parents slept in the bedroom down the hall from where the Nintendo was. Nick had good parents, and they wanted us in bed at a reasonable hour.

Nick's mom and dad put more energy into raising their son than my father did.

Probably because of that, Nick's dad scared the shit out of me.

When Nick's dad rumbled down the hallway and told us to go sleep, I closed my eyes and pretended to snore. Nick negotiated with his father in the doorway until his dad either agreed to let us stay up another half hour or yelled loud enough that we'd have to pretend to go to bed. Both Nick and his father could be extremely stubborn. Their negotiations were often heated.

Nick and I learned to play video games quietly. When we opened cans of Mountain Dew, we muffled the sound with paper towels. If it were a long weekend or the summer and Nick's parents had to wake up for work in the morning, we pretended to be asleep from around 5:30-6:30 so we wouldn't be caught.

And in this way, we played a great deal of Nintendo. After my great-grandmother bought me a Super Nintendo for Christmas, we played that.

I'd ride my bike to Nick's house. I brought my Super Nintendo with. I carried it in my backpack.

Incidentally, my great-grandmother, we called her Gammy, was extremely Norwegian, incredibly white. She never could quite figure out my Jew-for-Jesus of a freak father. Once, when I was a little boy, she took me aside at Thanksgiving and said, "Sammy, you must promise never to become a fat Russian Jew boy like your father."

I told Nick what my great-grandmother said about Jews and he laughed like a fool. And because he laughed, I was free to tell him something else she said.

"Did you know that Asian people eat poop?"

Gammy told my cousin and I this when we were children. Gammy was sure that Asian people used poop as fertilizer. This offended her. I told Nick about Gammy's warning, and he cackled and cackled.

Nick and I rented the game *Final Fantasy II* regularly. Later, after Japanese versions of the games were re-released in North America, this became *Final Fantasy V*. As seventh graders, something about the game fascinated and challenged us. So we played it. Too much.

Long after Nick killed himself, I kept his saved game on the cartridge that was buried in storage. Nick leveled everyone in his party up to level 99. For anybody who has played this game, you understand the time and energy that task requires. Impressive. I can't bring myself to get rid of this video game. Years later, it feels like a connection to Nick.

Incidentally, the cartridge I still have is labeled *Tecmo Super Bowl.* This is because Nick became adept at disassembling Super Nintendo cartridges from video rental stores. He'd switch out the circuit boards with games we had grown tired of playing. This allowed us to keep games that required time to beat such as *Final Fantasy II.* We did this for years and never got caught. Nick was one clever bastard.

Anyway, one night we were playing *Final Fantasy II.* Having worked tirelessly, one of us finally beat the game. It was three in the morning. At first, we were delirious with triumph. Then we were sick with boredom. So we came up with an idea.

There were these fluffy little white creatures called Moodles in the game. One of the things that a Moodle allowed you to do was to change your character's name. We thought it would be funny to swap the names of characters in order to switch their genders. We used profane words to others. Fuckface and shithead. Real clever.

Our epilogue of *Final Fantasy II* was full of gay marriages, and irreverent dialogue. This was hilarious to us. Boys were marrying boys, girls were marrying girls, and the whole game became a jumbled and incestuous orgy. This was even funnier to us because it was four in the morning, and we were trying to stay quiet so that Nick's parents wouldn't wake up. The more we tried not to laugh, the more we laughed.

By this time at night, I'd put away about half of a case of Mountain Dew. The only bathroom was next door to Nick's parent's room. So I was trying to hold it. Nick and I were howling like fools, and I was trying to control my bladder. Finally, the floodgates let go. Sitting there watching our mangled version of the ending of *Final*

Fantasy II, I laughed so hard that I pissed my pants.

Through my laughter, I turned to Nick and told him as much. He couldn't contain himself. He started laughing even harder.

Nick and I howled like fools as the game played itself out, as I sat wallowing in my own urine, and as Nick's parents pretended to sleep in the room down the hall.

Later, Nick let me borrow a pair of shorts. We learned to start going to the bathroom in the yard outside Nick's front door in the middle of the night so as not to wake his parents.

***

I'd like to take a moment to drift even further back in my memory to a friend who came before Nick. His name was Jordan.

When I was seven, I cared about Jordan as fiercely as I cared about Nick. This was in 1987, before my father scammed his way into the suburban neighborhood where Nick lived. We lived happily in an affluent neighborhood in St. Paul, before Dad divorced Mom and the bank foreclosed on our Tudor house near the Mississippi river.

Beneath that façade of happiness, Mom and Dad screamed at each other, smoked too much pot, and never felt safe to me. At an early age, I learned to wander down the street and hang out at Jordan's house.

Jordan's mom was a New Jersey fire-siren, but his father was a quiet man with a beard. Their house was calm and Jordan and I would play with our He-Man action figures in the basement. I remember that Jordan was small like me, quick to laugh, and enjoyed my company as much as I enjoyed his.

When we were seven, Jordan and I packed a lunch and attempted to travel to boogie land.

It was a warm summer's day. Jordan and I spent most of that summer at his house or at my house. Mostly we

29

pretended to be He-Man, chased each other around, and wasted time.

It was wonderful.

One day we decided to climb a pipe that ran up the outside of my house. We figured this pipe would take us to a magical land filled with boogers. Thus, boogie land. We told my mom. She was so amused that she packed us a lunch.

I remember looking up at the pipe with Jordan. In my memory, we stood staring up into the sun that obscured some distant and magical space between spaces. We didn't know where we were going, but we tried to go anyway.

I don't remember what happened next. It is hard to remember things that are so far away.

Time has since moved quickly, you know?

I do remember that, as early as seven years old, I had an insatiable wanderlust. Not so much for geographical locations, more for imaginative or spiritual planes of being. At seven, I wanted to be magical in my traveling. And I did not want to travel alone. I wanted Jordan to come with me.

Jordan moved to New Jersey at the end of that summer and I never saw him again. I suppose, like Nick, he is still out there somewhere.

After all, as I learned in writing this ceremony for Nick, once something is conjured, it does not go away.

***

Now I would like to mention a friendship that came after my relationship with Jordan and Nick. This was my friend Josh.

Josh and I were friends with Nick in middle school. When we weren't hanging out in Nick's basement or my basement, Nick and I could usually be found at Josh's house. Josh's parents were as kind to me as Nick's were. While my father was smoking pot at home, they provided another calm space for me to be.

Josh and I remained friends as we drifted into adulthood. This was because Josh never put a bullet in his brain.

Josh was tall, gawky, and had curly black hair. His last name was Twohy. So after Nick was done making fun of me for being a short, Russian Jew, and I was done making fun of his slanty eyes, we would call Josh a French fairy.

The three of us were great friends. In fact, Josh called me to let me know that Nick had killed himself. Josh even spoke before me at Nick's funeral.

"I can't believe it," he had said. Josh was in shock.

Though Nick and I used to laugh like fools at Josh for his atrocious spelling and grammar, Josh was one of the smartest people I've met. He was solving special calculus equations that our teacher had to invent for him by our junior year in high school. Even though he struggled with spelling as an adolescent, he was an avid reader. As seventh graders, he, Nick, and I devoured the *Sword of Shannara* series in a matter of days.

I've always depended on my friends and their families. My parents offered little in the way of support and so I would take my problems to them. So when I was thirty-two, I asked Josh to help me with my book about Nick.

He made a self-effacing reply.

"What, do you want me to spell check the thing?" He wore a mischievous smile.

I laughed.

"No," I said, "I want you to help me organize the chaos of the things that spew from my mind."

Do you know that Josh read the entire first draft of this book? I am talking about two hundred single spaced pages of chaos.

I didn't know how to write before I started writing this book about Nick. I still might not be much of a writer. But I'm trying. For Nick.

Josh cared a great deal about Nick. He also cared about

me. The feeling was mutual.

In fact, during our senior year of high school, Josh, Nick, and I parked my 1984 Oldsmobile Cutlass Cierra near a lake in our suburban neighborhood, north of St. Paul. It was two in the morning. It was 1997. We were smoking cigars. Josh was tall and skinny. He was sitting shotgun. Always shorter than everybody else, I was pushed up against the steering wheel. Nick was in the backseat, lightning our cigars for us. That night, we told each other that we loved each other. Not in a gay way, we were quick to point out, but in a friend way.

Nick wouldn't even tell his parents that he loved them. That is how much the three of us cared about each other.

***

I've had many close friends. Nick was one of my closest.

Ten years after he and I laughed about Magic's press conference in 1992, Nick put a bullet in his brain.

Ten years after that, in the fall of 2011, I got married.

Nick kept coming to me in my dreams. I kept going to him in my writing. Where are dreams? Where is writing? Perhaps I was still seeking boogie land? This time I was searching with Nick?

So I started putting together this book as a ceremony for him. In talking with Josh at my wedding, I learned that Nick had been coming to him in his dreams too. Whatever sort of boogie land Nick was in now, it felt as though he needed some help. So I asked Josh to help me with my writing project. I realized that this book was a vessel for *us* to get *there*. I was trying to take *us* to boogie land as a way to figure out Nick's death ten years after he pulled the trigger.

Talk about a project, right?

- CHAPTER 3 -

Earvin Johnson was born in July of 1979. He was a poor black boy in a rich white neighborhood. His father named him after his favorite basketball player, Earvin 'Magic' Johnson.

"This boy is going places," Earvin's father told Earvin's mother. His grin stretched from ear to ear.

***

Or how about this?

Magic was born when I was thirty-two. Though I didn't know it at the time, I needed a psychopomp to help me travel through an enormous, complicated universe in order to reach my friend Nick. Without Magic, I couldn't see Nick clearly. Magic helped me release Nick's soul by transforming the bullet Nick had shot into his head into a golden basketball, soaring as a perfect shot of energy through space to its destination.

I needed Magic to help *us* get *there*.

So Magic was a product of my imagination, my writing.

Okay.

***

Let's add this.

Magic 'Fucking' Johnson was born for real when he was struck by lightning a second time. The bolt hit him directly in the head. It took him somewhere.

In that glorious place, he met *them*. And he realized that he was *them*. And *they* smiled and told him that he needed to return.

"You are going places, Earvin," *they* told him, "*you* are Magic."

He returned to our world.

Like me, he had written a book to share what he learned with you, with *us*.

Magic had been hit by lightning twice and something inside of him came to life.

Two people I loved very much put bullets in their brains. Two suicides? Something inside of me came to life.

I didn't know what it was.

***

The following is an excerpt from the self-help, cult classic *I Was Struck By Lightning Twice, So So Were You!* by Magic 'Fucking' Johnson. If you were listening to this as audiobook, the voice reading the words would sound very much like a note being conjured by a flute.

"*They* were glowing. And when *they* spoke, it was like I was speaking. And I didn't want *them* to stop. I wanted *them* to speak with me like that forever. It was like a mess of music reverberating through my whole body. I'd never felt so alive. I was connected. And when *they* spoke to me and I listened (or was it me speaking and *them* listening?), I felt like *they* were giving me *their* glow.

They told me that I don't have to worry about death, that nothing every really dies.

They told me that I'd be okay. *They* told me that I'd always been okay and would always be okay.

They told me that I had always been, would always be, and would continue to keep becoming. *They* told me that *we* were doing it together.

I gotta tell you, people, that was some good magic when *we* was talking to each other. When the conversation stopped, when I woke up in a hospital room, I felt the warmth of real electricity in the pit of my stomach, none of that fluorescent stuff.

A nurse came into my room. She dropped my chart on the linoleum floor.

"Mr. Johnson, are you okay?"

"I am great, ma'am, never been better."

"Are you sure? Um… Well… Mr. Johnson, you seem to be glowing."

"Ma'am, I do believe you are right. Well how about this, then? I am Magic 'Fucking' Johnson, ma'am, so so are you."

The nurse stared at me with an open mouth.

That was when I took my new name. That was when I started playing this game for real. That was when I started living.

I had become a traveler.

We were going places.

***

"Sam," Magic told me as I traveled to him in my dreams, "you gotta keep writing."

"Why?" I asked him.

"I'm taking you somewhere, baby."

Okay.

My writing was so weird. But I let it keep happening. Something was emerging. Writing and dreaming became interconnected. Something was being conjured.

I dreamed about Nick that night, after writing about Magic in my classroom that morning.

***

"Nick, what's it like being dead?"

Nick didn't say anything. But I could see that he was thinking something, he just didn't know how to say it. When Nick didn't know how to say something, he didn't say it.

As he often did, Nick lit a cigarette. After inhaling deeply, he let loose a perfectly formed smoke ring. Nick's smoke rings were always precisely constructed.

"You want to play Nintendo, Sam?"

I always wanted to play Nintendo. Since I didn't know

36

how to get Nick to talk about being dead, I followed him inside his house instead. We bounced down the stairs to his basement. Nick ignored his mom as she called after him.

"Nick, are you home now?"

He slammed the door as we entered the basement. I turned on the TV.

"Baseball Stars?"

I loved Baseball Stars. So we turned on the Nintendo. Both he and I had teams we had been building. Nick had a female shortstop named Hotty. She was completely maxed out. She hit a homerun every time she came to the plate. And she was hot.

I had a first-basement named Fatty. He was maxed out for power but had zero for speed. If he didn't hit it out of the park, he usually got thrown out at first. But he usually hit it out of the park. And he was fat.

Both Nick and I laughed when Fatty came to the plate.

Both Nick and I leered when Hotty came to the plate.

We played against each other. Hotty was at bat. My pitcher struck her out. I gave credit to Fatty for calling the pitches. Like he often had when we were kids, Nick got so frustrated that he slammed the controller into the ground. It smashed into bits and pieces.

Nick took the bits and pieces and puts them back together. He has done this before. Sometimes he got so angry that he smashed his fist into the ground. He broke his knuckle doing that once.

I wasn't afraid of Nick.

Though I knew Nick was capable of great emotion, he had lashed out at me physically only once.

We were in seventh grade. We were playing NHL '94 at our friend Dan's house. I scored a game-winning goal. Nick was pissed.

I was sitting on the couch in Dan's living room. Nick was on the floor. He leapt at me. Nick hit me so hard that my glasses dug into my face. I started to bleed. I was shocked. I ended up in the bathroom. I cried a little bit. I didn't let Nick or Dan know that I cried.

I could tell that Nick felt terrible about what he had done. He could see that I was upset. We didn't say anything about it. We kept playing video games.

That was the only time Nick's rage caused him to hurt me. He usually hurt himself instead. Whether punching his fist into the ground, slamming his foot into the carpet, or firing a bullet into his head, Nick was usually the target of his own frustration. I always figured he cared about people too much to lash out at them. I suppose what his suicide did to his parents complicated the sentence I just wrote. Nick's parents were devastated.

Anyway, Nick put the controller back together with super glue and we finished the game of Baseball Stars. I let him win. And then his mother came downstairs. She told me that it was time to leave.

I looked at Nick. Nick looked at me. Neither of us spoke. Then I disappeared.

I woke up.

***

But because of what I had written, Magic remained in my place.

***

Sam disappeared. He returned to that space where time moved quickly. His alarm clock snatched him. And he was busy again kissing his wife, making plays with high school kids, paying bills, and racing from one adult task to another.

This left Magic and Nick alone in that space between spaces.

It was then that Nick took notice of Magic.

"Are you glowing?" Nick asked.

Magic smiled.

"Where are we?" Nick was confounded.

"We ain't nowhere yet, baby." Magic laughed.

Nick was awake now. There was an ache in his head. He didn't know why. A confusing blankness surrounded him.

Magic reached out his hand. Nick looked at it absently.

"Ain't you gonna shake my hand?" Magic held the glowing hand out patiently.

"Am I gonna catch that glow?" Nick growled with sarcasm.

"I wish it were that easy, baby." Magic laughed even harder.

Nick shrugged. He acquiesced and shook Magic's hand. A tingle came through his body. He winced.

"The name is Magic 'Fucking' Johnson."

Despite his gruff demeanor, Nick laughed. Magic kept shaking Nick's hand.

"What is your name?"

Something dawned on Nick.

"Nicholas Louis Wiseman?" Nick asked.

He paused and looked around. There was something he was trying to remember. He laughed again as he fixed his gaze on Magic.

"What the hell kinda name is Magic 'Fucking' Johnson?" Nick asked.

"It is the kind of name that is gonna help us get out of here." Magic referred to the blankness around them.

"What is wrong with here?" Nick's response was immediate, automatic.

"It isn't *there*, that's what's wrong."

"Bullshit, you jackass," Nick released Magic's hand.

Magic howled with laughter.

"We got some traveling to do Nick, that is for sure."

Nick's hand reached up to his head. Something was wrong. He wasn't sure what.

There was an electric charge in the air. It felt to Nick as

though lightning were about to strike.

- CHAPTER 4 -

My wife Katie and I were married in the fall of 2011. Nick's parents attended that ceremony.

Katie and I only invited 70 people. The people that were there were important to us. Nick's parents are family.

Pete and Daphne Wiseman were like parents to me when I was twelve and thirteen and fourteen. They fed me dinner, talked to me about school, and treated me with warmth and kindness.

My father often ignored me. Pete and Daphne noticed me. As Nick slammed his bedroom door and told his parents to leave us alone, I rolled my eyes and smiled consolingly at them. Then I followed Nick into his bedroom and played video games with him. Knowing what I know about bad parents, I can say the following without hesitation. Pete and Daphne were good parents.

Pete and Daphne were Midwesterners from humble backgrounds. Though I never summoned the courage to ask them directly, I always assumed they were unable to have children of their own. I figured this was why they adopted Nick.

Pete injured his hip in a motorcycle crash. This injury left him with a noticeable limp. Pete was very much a cop. He knew what to do with weapons, had a fierce sense of justice, and was willing to extend his authority when necessary.

I stayed in touch with Nick's parents after Nick killed himself. Daphne came out and watched many of the plays that I wrote and directed. We exchanged emails every so often.

So I invited them to my wedding and was proud to have them there.

Katie and I were married in the backyard of her cousin's house in Minneapolis. It was an intimate ceremony.

After the wedding ceremony, Pete and Daphne were standing in the street.

Pete stood silently in a plaid suit from the 70's. He was

smoking a cigarette, sending perfectly formed smoke rings to the sky. It was a sunny, October morning. Daphne was standing next to him. I shook Pete's hand and gave Daphne a hug.

My sister Christie smoked as well, so she approached Pete to bum a cigarette.

Christie is four years older than me. She's managed to bum her way through life. Whether begging money from Dad, pawning my bike when I was in middle school, or even panhandling after she ran away from home at sixteen, she somehow managed to keep traveling through this enormous, complicated universe.

Though you would never be able to tell, Christie has cerebral palsy. This was because she was born four months premature in 1976. Unlike our three siblings who didn't survive, Christie did.

My parent's first child was a miscarriage. Their second child made it to the final term and was even named Jayson when he died. Christa was the third child. She lived for a week before passing away. My sister Christie was born four months premature in 1976.

Dad prayed over that baby for months. Though he was Jewish, he did so in the name of Jesus. So when she survived, they named her Christie. And because she survived, my parents decided to try and make me.

To hear my mom speak of it, I came out perfect. I was in a bubble of water. It was a Caesarean section.

Mom does speak of it. In fact, she won't shut up about it. Unlike Nick's mom and dad, my mom can't help but to share every intimate detail of her life story with whoever will listen. This embarrassed me as a child. In retrospect, this might be one reason Mom survived Jim's suicide. She'd run up to strangers in the grocery store and start blabbering about the bullet her husband put in his brain. Though it horrified her audiences, it let out the great emotional energies caught up inside of her. This was in contrast to Pete and Daphne's private stoicism. They'd hardly mention Nick's name anymore.

Anyway, my parents named my sister Christie because of Christ. They named me Samuel because of the prophet. In Hebrew, Sh'muel means God Listens.

My parents believed that God listened to their prayers and that was where I came from.

And here I am. And there I was, watching Christie smoke with Nick's dad.

My sister started to talk to Pete. When I told her that Pete was Nick's father, her eyes got wide.

Christie, like her father, smoked too much pot. Also like her father, she was clueless when it came to social cues. She didn't have any sense that Nick's dad didn't want to talk about Nick.

"You are Nick's dad? Hey! I remember Nick! He was that Asian kid that used to play video games with Sam! I am so sorry. That sucks what he did."

She smelled of cigarettes. Christie was wearing a sweatshirt. Skylar, her thirteen year-old son, stood with us. Overweight and embarrassed by her appearance, she shifted her weight with a sort of naïve enthusiasm when she remembered Nick.

Mr. Wiseman stared at her. His face was expressionless. Discomfort radiated from him. After a moment of silence, he said this.

"Pretty nice weather we are having, right?"

***

Katie and I were married at the end of October. We scheduled a brief ceremony and reception over the MEA fall break at our schools. In Minnesota, schools take a two-day break in the fall. I taught high school and Katie taught elementary. So we figured that would be a good time to squeeze in a wedding.

Had he not put a bullet in his brain, Nick would have been my best man.

Instead, my good friends Josh and Mike stood with me as I said, "I do."

The wedding pictures were funny. Both Josh and Mike are over six feet tall. Josh has dark hair and Mike is a blonde. And I was five foot nothing, standing between the two of them. Looking at the pictures afterwards reminded me of struggling to figure out how to play with them on the basketball court. What I lacked in size, I made up for in tenacity. But I was still pretty terrible.

Nick was also five foot nothing. Watching him play taught me how to play guard. He was so damned tenacious.

Anyway, Dad performed my wedding ceremony.

I asked him to do this. My father had one of those online minister certificates at the time. He kept his ministry licensed the same way that he kept his insurance business up and running. Underneath tables.

My father was raised an orthodox Jew by his Russian immigrant parents. He became a born-again Christian after his buddy Dave came back from Vietnam with a bible. Dave annoyed my dad until he agreed to pray in the name of Jesus about something.

Dave was a nerd. He wore black-rimmed glasses and pocket protectors. He was tall, gangly, and something of a Puritan. His four children weren't allowed to watch television. So when Dave brought his family over to our house, it was something of game for my sister and I to contaminate them with Super Mario, Nickelodeon, or profanity.

"Say shit," my sister would prod.

"Do it!" I chimed in.

Dave's kids would get nervous and watch the clock until they got to return to the safety of their own home.

Dave was the best classical guitar player I ever met. When his agile fingers manipulated the strings, the notes came out like perfectly formed notes, conjured by a flute. Or how about this? They emerged like perfectly formed smoke rings.

Anyway, the something my dad agreed to pray in the name of Jesus about was his mom. Dad's mother, my bubbe, had recently been given shock therapy to deal with her nerves. I imagine her anxiety might have something to do with being chased out of Russia as a child because she was Jewish, losing her mother in the process, and ending up in poverty on the lower east side of St. Paul. Being struck by lightning is a much different thing than being zapped by doctors. And zap her they did. According to my father, each treatment left his mother more and more neurotic, anxious, and unsettled. This happened for months. The shock therapy didn't work.

The prayer did. Work, that is. The next day my bubbe was released from the hospital, had a date with a man she knew from high school, and to hear my father speak of it, returned from the dead.

So my grandmother kicked her depression and my dad became a Jew for Jesus. This was all before I was born. And that is one of the reasons my dad got his minister's certificate. Dave believed in Jesus so so did you, right?

Dave played guitar at my wedding. He had also played at my dad's first wedding nearly forty years earlier. Mom and Dad made it fourteen years before their divorce when I was seven. Dave played *The Wedding Song* by Pete Stookey at both their wedding and my own.

The wedding ceremony marked the only time that my mom, my dad, my sister and I were together after my parent's divorce. It had been twenty-four years since we had been a family in that Tudor house in St. Paul.

Mom and Dad wanted to walk down the aisle with me. It was the first time both of them stood at my side since I was a little boy.

As we were walking down the aisle, Mom started to cry. So did I. So did Dad.

I was holding her up. She was seventy pounds. She was six months removed from finding her husband on the floor of the garage.

Jim, like Nick, had put a bullet in his brain.

Mom had issues with anorexia dating back to her childhood. She also had issues with drugs and with alcohol. So she looked as though she were 100 years old at the wedding even though she was sixty-two. This was self-induced. A couple of months after the ceremony, Mom was kicked out of the assisted living facility that she was placed in after Jim's suicide. She refused to stop smoking in her apartment the same way she refused to let her sister Polly and I help her with her finances or support her through the aftermath of Jim's death.

Anyway, Mom the recovering alcoholic managed to sneak half a bottle of wine from the bar after the ceremony, during our reception. And she didn't care for the Thai food that we served so she ate eight cupcakes. Like Nick, Mom was tenacious.

My father was tenacious as well. He spent much of my childhood proselytizing me. After much prompting, I prayed in the name of Jesus for my something. Dad and I had gone for a walk by the Mississippi river and we ended up on a bench looking over the water. Dad often took me for walks with him. Whether or not he was stoned, those were my favorite times with him.

Dad told me that I could pray in the name of Jesus for anything that I wanted and it would come true. Talk about magic.

So I thought about it and I decided that I wanted to pray for my mom and my sister. I wanted God to take care of them because I didn't know if they could take care of themselves. I was seven years old.

It worked. It was twenty-four years between that prayer and my wedding. In that time Region's hospital in St. Paul had all but pronounced my mom dead twice. She'd survived a broken neck, a pickled liver, and her husband's suicide to make it to the day of my wedding.

After walking me down the aisle, Dad presided over a

strange wedding ceremony. The ritual was a deconstruction of a traditional Christian and Jewish ceremony. Much to my delight, my wife Katie's Catholic family wasn't overly horrified when my father made fun of the drudgery and mysticism of Catholic weddings. Instead, they laughed at his jokes. They appreciated the intimacy of the ceremony. I did too. Dad did a great job.

Prior to the occasion, I spent about a month trying to make my father script the event. He wouldn't. Or so I thought. I soon realized that he couldn't. For my father, improvisation wasn't a luxury. It was a necessity. That is the way he worked.

My father, for better or worse, has let his life come to him.

"How about this, Dad?" I emailed a script I wrote for the ceremony. He had since retired in Florida.

"Don't worry about it, Sam, I'll say whatever comes to me," he responded.

I gnashed my teeth and stopped trying to push him to prepare. So the wedding ceremony ran wild.

Katie's family and mine were gathered for a moment. Mike, Josh, and I stood in front of Nick's parents as my dad conducted the ritual connecting Katie and I. All of *us* were *there*.

As I read my vows, I told Katie that this ceremony marked the end of the dysfunction of the family that I came from. It was a transition into my new family. I cried as I told my new wife this in front of our family and friends, in front of *them*.

As much as I meant to communicate a cut with where I had come from to where I was going at the time, I learned through conducting *this* ceremony for Nick that once something is conjured, it doesn't go away. Katie seemed to have a sense of this all along. Her emotional intelligence is staggering. And she loves me even though my family is strange. So when we kissed at the end of the ceremony, we meant it.

Incidentally, the final bit of the improvised ceremony involved the crushing of a wine class. My father still had the original glass that he had bought for him and my mother to crush forty years prior. Due to a mix-up, they hadn't crushed the glass at the time. This might be an explanation for their three lost children, my premature sister, and their nasty divorce. It might not. Anyway, my father had poured too much wine into the glass that we needed to crush. So he made a joke and gulped it in front of our family and friends. And they laughed. And so did I. And so did Katie.

I stomped on the glass, it shattered into a million pieces, and Katie and I were married.

***

My friend Mike got married a year after I did. Had Nick not put a bullet in his brain, he would have been in that wedding party with me. Pete and Daphne Wiseman were invited. Unlike my wedding, they didn't make it.

You see, Mr. and Mrs. Wiseman had finally sat down to watch the German videos that Nick, Josh, and I made in our high school German class.

After seeing the first image of his son in ten years, Pete couldn't summon the courage to come see one of Nick's close friends from high school get married. So Pete and Daphne were too overcome with grief to come to Mike's ceremony.

It was the fall of 2012. The wedding party sat in the staging area as Mike was getting ready to say I do.

Mike was extremely Nordic. He had piercing, Aryan eyes. He was about to marry a tall, blonde, Nordic girl who also had piercing, Aryan eyes.

When we were kids, I used to joke that Mike's tall, blonde, Aryan children would probably put my short, Jewish children in camps. This was back before Nick put a bullet in his brain. And so Nick would listen to my joke and cackle like a fool.

Then we would make a joke about Nick's slanty-eyed children. All of us would howl with laughter.

Anyway, long after Nick blew his brains out long before he could have those slanty-eyed children, a crowd was gathering outside for Mike's wedding.

Mike had just finished reading a draft of my book about Nick. So he turned to me, a groomsman, and said that he had watched the 30 for 30 special on Earvin "Magic" Johnson's HIV announcement. He turned to me with a mischievous smile.

"Magic faced it like a man," Mike told me, "he owned up to it and held a news conference immediately after he found out."

I smiled. Mike looked so nervous in his tuxedo. He was finally settling down much like I had finally settled down. Nick, incidentally, never settled down. He chose a bullet instead of a wedding ceremony.

I digress.

"You know the funny thing, Sam?" Mike was looking past the groomsmen that were scattered around the waiting area in an office complex made out of Marble. His eyes were out the window, scanning the audience that was gathering in the outdoor amphitheatre.

"What?"

"HIV didn't phase Magic, but marriage scared the shit out of him."

I laughed like a fool as Mike spit his gum out into the garbage in order to go outside and get married.

***

Six months prior to my wedding, I had dinner at Nick's house for the first time in nearly ten years.

After inviting Pete and Daphne to attend my wedding, Daphne sent me an email. She suggested that Josh and I come over for dinner. She wanted to meet my fiancé

Katie. She also wanted see Josh's newborn daughter.

So nearly ten years after Nick's suicide, Josh and I were returning to his house for the first time since we'd come together before Nick's funeral. About eight of us guys, Nick's friends, gathered at the house. Nick's dad gave us porcelain figurines of a little white dog that morning. This was meant to symbolize Nick's dog Willie. Willie may have been Nick's favorite thing in the universe. He loved that dog fiercely.

Anyway, Mrs. Wiseman told Josh that she had something to give him the night of our dinner. He was sure that it was the copies of the German videos that the three of us made in high school. Josh was ecstatic. He had been trying to get his hands on them for years.

"As much as they are Nick's, they are also ours," he told me.

We were joking with each other after we rang the doorbell.

"If she doesn't give us the videos, one of us has to sneak into the basement and find them."

"We could come back later and break in."
"Do you still remember the garage code?"

"Nick used to climb up onto the deck, remember that?"

"I am too old for that."

"Me too."

Josh and I were sort of serious and sort of kidding.

We kept talking.

"Isn't it weird that they never moved?"
"If my kid did that, I would sell the house immediately."

"What do you think they have in Nick's room now?"

"Do you think the body is still down there?"

Josh smiled obscenely. I laughed.

Josh's wife admonished us and Katie rolled her eyes.

After the suicide, we had not been allowed into Nick's room. Both Josh and I arrived early that morning after they found Nick. The first thing Pete said, smoking a cigarette on the front steps, was that we shouldn't go in Nick's bedroom.

So it had been years since we had been down to the basement where Nick's bedroom was. We spent much our adolescence there.

Mrs. Wiseman opened the front door and we shut up.

Inside the house, the first thing I noticed was that there was the head of a dead animal in the foyer. It was a beast.

"I thought you made Pete keep his trophy's in the basement?" I asked Mrs. Wiseman after she hugged me.

She laughed.

"It wouldn't fit down there," she said.

"It is a Kudo," Pete said. He voice was thick with a smoker's cough.

"Pete and I went to Africa two years ago."

"I've always wanted to go big game hunting." Pete was standing at the top of the stairs. Mr. and Mrs. Wiseman lived in a split-level townhome. When Nick was alive, he claimed the basement. They lived upstairs.

Josh and I asked about their trip. We talked as they finished cooking dinner.

"Those sons of bitches will get you unless you get them first," Mr. Wiseman handed Josh and I a beer. He was referring to big game. Sons of bitches.

"If something like that thing on the wall were coming at me, I'd want Mr. Wiseman there," Josh joked.

"I'd *need* him there," I said.

We laughed.

Later, when Mr. Wiseman was having a cigarette on the deck, Mrs. Wiseman confided in me.

"I swear that sometimes, when I am having a glass of wine on the couch, I can see that trophy wink at me."

She was talking about the Kudo.

Mrs. Wiseman was anti-gun, anti-hunting, and decidedly liberal. This was in opposition to her husband, the gun toting, hunting, conservative.

After Mr. Wiseman came back inside, I asked them

about their dogs, Willie and Yoda.

"We had to put Willie down last year, Yoda has been gone for a couple of years now."

"You didn't want to get new dogs?" I asked.

"No." And that was that.

A picture of Nick from high school was prominently displayed on the mantle. A storybook he had written in third grade was next to it. Even though he was surrounding us, Nick's name wasn't mentioned, not even once.

The basement door was shut. Nick's room was closed off to us. That is where Josh and I spent countless hours in their house. In the basement, as well as in the driveway outside, playing touch football.

Though he was the reason we were all sitting there, we didn't say a word about Nick.

As we were leaving, Mrs. Wiseman gave Josh a bottle of wine instead of the German videos. He blamed me.

"What the hell was that?"

"Why didn't you ask for the German videos?"

"I was waiting for you."

"Shit."

"Yes, shit."

As we were driving home from the dinner, I told Katie about Nick's parents.

"Wasn't that was weird?" she asked me.

"What?"

"That we didn't even mention Nick?"

"I guess it was."

And I went on to tell her that, during middle school, I would ride the bus home with Nick. His parents cooked me dinner nearly every night. They provided me with stability. They listened to me when I talked. Their dinner table was one of the first places where people took what I had to say seriously.

They cared about me.

Having dinner with them reminded me how important

they were to me. As I told them about my work as a teacher, as a doctoral student, I remembered what Pete and Daphne had offered me as a kid. It reminded me how important Nick was to me.

The support of Nick's parents was one of the reasons I was able to keep traveling through this enormous, complicated universe.

So I told Katie that. I told Josh. Both of them told me to share what I was thinking with Pete and Daphne.

So I sent an email that said as much later on that week.

They were touched. Daphne agreed to have lunch with me. Later, she sent an email to let Josh and I know that she was interested in watching the German video with us. She had not been able to bring herself to see an image of Nick yet.

I suggested that her and Pete come over to my house in Northeast Minneapolis and we make a night out of it. She agreed.

But as much as Josh and I were opening up with the Wisemans, I couldn't bring myself to tell her about my writing. Not only was this book starting to happen, I wrote a play about Nick at the time as well.

They were so hurt by what Nick had done. I didn't know if they could handle the funeral ceremony I was dreaming up.

I knew that it was important to share it with them. That email was a first step.

Finishing this book with them in mind was another.

- C H A P T E R 5 -

Dinosaurs
Run
Wild.

It was passing time. I was traveling to my classroom to teach. It was between second and third period. A high school teacher has to be strategic in order to use the bathroom.

Once again, I'd spent the morning writing about Nick.

I bobbed and weaved through a crowded hallway. The students were like cattle on the march from room to room.

Incidentally, I took the previous line from a musical I wrote about high school. In it, there was a song about how students are forced to behave like obedient cattle.

The reviewers were not amused with my critique of school. In fact, after watching a performance, one critic wrote that watching the play was like having a lobotomy with a jackhammer.

Writing is hard.

Anyway, in the ten years that I have taught high school, I have learned to be wily as I move through school hallways. I travel like Magic Johnson, baby.

I am only a smidge over five feet tall, a pinch over 130 pounds, and a nonconforming thinker. So I've learned to be careful in schools, especially crowded hallways. In fact, walking through a school hallway is similar to navigating a crowd at a concert.

I find openings and push through them politely. I can leave my spot in front of the stage, hit the bathroom, and get back before Bob Pollard finishes *Game of Pricks*. I have tested this claim at First Avenue in Minneapolis.

I've learned to navigate the masses of humanity as they move from place to place. I dare say that I'm pretty good at it.

So it was something of a shock when I felt Vicky push past me as I was walking from second period to third period. She found the opening before I could. She traveled by. As she did, I observed two things.

First, Vicky was wearing a wedding veil.

Second, Vicky was being followed.

The wedding veil was easy to spot. Evidence for my

second inference came when I heard her say the following.

"Save me Mr. Tanner, Ms. Stone is after me!"

Here is a brief description of Vicky. She was a sophomore. She was a Hispanic, white-hipster hybrid. She was a smidge over five feet tall. I had her in my drama workshop class as a freshman. She took my second drama workshop course the next year. This was probably because my class was one of the only in the school that let Vicky do things such as wear wedding veils, find openings to push through, or express her abstract creativity in positive ways. I never assigned a worksheet, forced her to sit in a desk, or gave her a multiple choice test.

So it was unsurprising that Vicky was asking me to save her from the assistant principal. I'd been doing my part to save her from the standardized oppression of schools for as long as I'd known her.

Incidentally, that may have been one of the things that Nick rejected when he pulled the trigger, the standardized oppression of schools. He stopped turning in assignments when he was a sophomore. By senior year it was remarkable if he woke up with his alarm. Mike and I were in his carpool. We'd wait outside his house. If fifteen minutes passed and he didn't come out, we'd just head to school without him. When asked, Nick said that he would rather sleep than go to school.

In 8th grade, Nick was the top student in our class. By senior year, he had trouble walking through the front door of a school.

I digress.

"Vicky. Stop." I tried to play my part as a public educator in the employ of a school. I didn't really mean it.

Vicky did not stop. In fact, she kept going. And she traveled more quickly.

I saw that the assistant principal, Ms. Stone, was in hot pursuit. Ms. Stone was bobbing and weaving through the hallways far less effectively than Vicky or I. Bob Pollard would've been long finished with *Game of Pricks* if Ms.

Stone had needed to use the bathroom at the start of the song. *I am a Scientist*, too.

Ms. Stone, knowing that Vicky respected me (probably because I respected Vicky), asked me to make Vicky stop traveling.

I was trapped. I was caught between my intuitive respect for anybody who would run from the those who would squelch creativity (or demand that a student take a wedding veil off in order to conform to the hat policy in a school) and my role as a public educator in the employ of the general taxpayer by way of a team of administrators such as Ms. Stone. I did the only thing I could think to do.

I ignored the situation and walked into my classroom.

A minute passed, and I shuffled some papers on a table. I felt guilty for having left both Vicky and Ms. Stone in such obvious conflict. I don't like conflict. It is so violent. And I cared about both of these people.

So I popped my head back out into the hallway.

There was Ms. Stone pointing her finger at Vicky. And there was Vicky wearing a wedding veil in the hallways.

Ms. Stone, clearly confused, looked at me.

"Mr. Tanner, is this a drama thing?"

Oftentimes people have tried to understand the strange things that have happened in my presence.

"Sam, you are so funny!" People would tell me in my social life.

"Mr. Tanner, you are crazy!" My students would say.

"Mr. Tanner? He is our *drama* teacher," my colleagues would say, "you never know *what* he's going to do."

These are the more pleasant things people have said to make sense of me. There have been less pleasant interactions that I have experienced.

Anyway, I assured Ms. Stone that the veil on Vicky's head was most certainly not a drama thing.

Then the bell rang. And then I taught my third hour class. And then Vicky was suspended from school for a week for not following the hat policy.

High schools are such silly places.
There is very little room in them for easy traveling.

**

Vicky etched something into a desk in my classroom when she was enrolled in my drama workshop two course.

Vicky didn't scrawl profanity, she didn't draw genitalia, and she didn't come up with lewd insults. These are all things that I have scrubbed off desks at one point in my career or another. She did, however, draw a picture of a smiling dinosaur. And next to the dinosaur, she wrote the following phrase: Dinosaurs Run Wild.

Vicky was so weird! I loved it.

I sat down in that desk one morning, while I was writing this book. I opened my laptop before the students arrived. I preferred the openness of my empty classroom to the claustrophobia of my office behind the stage in my classroomroom. Sitting in Vicky's desk and dreaming up a ceremony for my friend Nick, I took notice of Vicky's piece of art.

Dinosaurs Run Wild?

"Yes, Vicky," I thought, "they do."

I took pause and thought. Dinosaurs were extinct. Their bones, like Nick's, were decaying beneath the earth. And to that point, all of our bones will someday be like Nick's.

And running wild was synonymous with traveling. It was the opposite of being stuck. It was what Magic 'Fucking' Johnson could do in my writing. It was what people were capable of when they unleashed their psyche and traveled. It was what happened when I open up my laptop and started tapping at keys. My mind began to run wild with powerful memories. Creative visions. Easy traveling became possible in the space of writing.

So the idea that dinosaurs could run wild was the idea that the dead could come back to life and travel. This meant that Earvin could be struck by lightning twice and come back as Magic 'Fucking' Johnson. This also meant that Nick could come and visit me in my dreams after he put a bullet in his brains. It also meant that all of the pain that we bury deep inside of ourselves could come back to life and run wild even if we tried to jam it into a coffin and bury it deep beneath the surface. It meant that we could easily travel through this pain and transform it into something positive if we found a space to do so.

This book, then, was also about dinosaurs running wild. In fact, it was a space where I let dinosaurs run wild.

***

So here is a story about dinosaurs running wild.

I observed student teachers as part of my doctoral work. I watched them teach English in high school classrooms and gave them notes. One of my student teachers was placed in the high school that Nick and I had attended.

I found myself, fifteen years after he and I had graduated, sitting in 12th grade English again.

An adult, I sat in a desk and watched an English class. I was on the outside looking in.

The students were reading *Man's Search for Meaning* by Viktor Fankl. In the book, Frankl tries to figure out his experience as a Jew in a concentration camp. He tries to come up with a reason to live.

Incidentally, Nick did not come up with a reason to live. That is why he shot himself with an assault rifle.

At the beginning of the class period, the student teacher reminded the class that they would not pass unless they turned in all of their essays. He also reminded them that many of them needed the class to graduate. After he said this, a couple of white students laughed and said the name Peter.

I watched the only Asian kid in the class turn to the

group of white students and smile at them. It was that same sort of mischievous smile Nick used to give me. Clearly, this was Peter. And Peter was in danger of failing the class.

Nick failed nearly every class he took his senior year.

As the class period progressed, Peter was engaged in a discussion about *Man's Search for Meaning*. He raised his hand and said intelligent things. He responded tactfully to the ideas that his peers offered up.

He seemed smart and he seemed pleasant. Though he was in danger of flunking out, he didn't care. He reminded me of Nick.

As the students were talking about how to find meaning, their conversation drifted to death.

Now I am going to try to paraphrase something that one of the students said. I am sad that I cannot cite him more directly, because his words affected me deeply.

"Maybe it doesn't matter if you realize that your life was important at the moment that you die. Maybe your life becomes important as other people realize why your life was important after you die. Maybe that is what makes your life and your death meaningful."

This statement conjured Nick for me.

As I wrote this book, maybe I started to realize how important Nick's life had been to me.

I looked mournfully at Peter, this Asian student in an all white classroom.

I kept it together through the observation and through my follow-up conversation with the student teacher. But when I got to my car, I cried my eyes out.

Nick, long extinct like a dinosaur, was running wild in me once more.

***

I wrote the following section in my classroom the next morning before my students arrived, because Nick was running wild inside of me. I was frustrated that I was so busy and that he wasn't.

Here is what I wrote.

Nick got out of work. He got out of being stuck in sixty-hour workweeks. That conniving bastard got out of driving to school in a snowstorm at 6:00 in the morning.

Nick got out of being thirty-two, got out of getting married, got out of getting older and getting tired, got out of worrying about bank accounts and mortgages and student loans and all of that colonizing bullshit.

In many ways, Nick was resisting the imperial touch of Western Civilization, its schools, its workplaces, its conventions, and its adulthood.

He didn't want to become what I have since become, a good white person.

One squeeze of the trigger and he, like the character Bartleby the Scrivener in the short story by the same name, told everybody that he would prefer not to.

Incidentally, I shared this with my high school students the last time that I taught Bartleby the Scrivener. I shared Nick with them as a way to think about the story. I did this because, due to this book, Nick was running wild in me.

About Bartleby.

Herman Melville created Bartleby. By that point in his life, Herman was at the end of his rope. Penniless and lonely, he was close to checking out.

I didn't create Nick. Nick was and is real. The version of him that shows up here is sort of my creation. But I'm writing down things as I remember them and as I know them. At one time, they felt very real to me. They still do. And that is why they show up here. Speaking of real, Nick was really good at getting out of school.

By junior year in high school he realized that, because his parents left for work so early in the morning, all he had to do was wait for them to leave, call the school pretending to be his dad, and fall back asleep. After getting in trouble a couple of times from his parents, Nick learned that if he got the mail before his parents came home from work, he could intercept the truancy letter that the school sent out. His parents wouldn't learn of his absence from school. That conniving bastard managed to miss most of his junior and senior year and still graduate.

I think his teachers took pity on him and gave him D's instead of F's. Nick was a likeable guy.

By my senior year, I was as sick of the conventions of school and the workplace as Nick. It became easier for Nick to convince me to skip school during lunch. When he'd say that we should just not go back for the second half of the day, I'd say yes again. And usually, after eating at Perkins or Applebees or something, we'd go back to his house. And we would turn on his Nintendo. We'd play the video game *Genghis Khan* on his Nintendo for hours. Rather than going to school and worrying about our grades or our future jobs, we'd trade resources, build armies, and try to take over the known world in the 14th century.

I loved playing *Genghis Khan* with Nick. I first encountered the game when I was ten or eleven. I'd play it in my room for hours. It was so complicated.

I introduced it to Nick some time during high school. During senior year, he and I got into matches that would last for months. I remember one game in particular. I took control of England. Nick took control of Japan.

Incidentally, Nick also took control of Asian nations when we played war games. He was the master of playing as imperial Japan in the board game version of Axis and Allies when we were in seventh grade.

Anyway, after hundreds of hours of game play, I had conquered the known world west of the Urals. Nick had conquered everything east of the Urals, and we were poised for an epic showdown between Western Civilization and the Eastern world.

Of course, as is the way with old Nintendo games, the saved game file became corrupted and our data was erased.

What a letdown.

The western and eastern worlds were never allowed to meet, as it were.

How fitting.

After senior year, Nick scammed his way into the University of Minnesota with me. We were admitted into the General College. The program, long since cut by the University, admitted students with high ACT scores and low GPA's. That was Nick and I. Nick got a 28 on his ACT. I got a 27. Nick's GPA was under two. Mine was a decimal point above.

Incidentally, at thirty-two I was halfway through my doctoral work. I was sitting pretty at a 4.0. I found irony there. Nick would have too. He would have laughed his ass off about that with me.

So Nick and I got into the University of Minnesota through the backdoor. And I worked my ass off that fall so that I could transfer into the College of Liberal Arts in the spring and become a real English major in a real college. I wanted to be respectable. Our friends Mike and Josh, my roommates during my freshmen year, were admitted into the University's Carlson School of Management and IT school, respectively. And talk about respected schools. And talk about the shit that they gave Nick and I for being rejects because we were in General College. They were on a fast track to respectable jobs, healthy paychecks, and successful living as defined by Western Civilization, its schools, its workplaces, its conventions, and its adulthood.

Maybe being an English major wasn't as prestigious, but at least it let me feel like I was a part of their world.

Nick, on the other hand, slacked his ass off, was on academic probation by the winter, and dropped out by the spring.

He looked the University of Minnesota square in the eye and, like Bartleby the Scrivener, told it that he preferred not to.

About four years later he put a bullet in his brain.

"I prefer not to," that gunshot said.

About ten years later, I woke up at 4:45 in the morning, kissed my wife on the cheek, got into my car, and drove through a blizzard to the high school that I teach in. I wrote about Nick all morning, taught all day, and drove to the University of Minnesota in the evening to take a class towards my PhD. All in all, I spent nearly sixteen hours working that day.

As I was driving through that blizzard, I thought about Nick. If we were eighteen and he were sitting next to me and we were on our way to class at the University, he'd have turned to me and told me that he didn't want to go.

And he'd have convinced me to ditch class, go back to his house, and play *Genghis Khan* all afternoon.

It would have been great.

***

Last night I fell asleep and I dreamed again. Nick's mom and dad had asked me to watch their house while they were away.

Nick's mom had a stern, white face. Nick's dad's mustache was carefully kept. Both of them looked out with perceptive eyes from behind a pair of thick glasses.

I told them that I would watch their house. As they were leaving, I began to get really nervous. What if Nick's ghost came to me at night? Wouldn't that be scary?

So I called Josh and asked him if he would come over and watch the house with me. I told him to bring his Playstation Three. I'd bring my XBOX 360. He and I, in that strange in-between space of being thirteen or being thirty-two that is allowed in that strange in-between space of dreaming and being unstuck, could play video games all night. We could keep each other company and ward off Nick's ghost.

Josh said maybe.

And then I was in Nick's house. I had to let his dogs Willy and Yoda out to piddle. That is what Nick's dad use to call it. He said the dogs had to piddle. But I knew that Willy and Yoda were dead. Yoda had died a couple of years ago and Willy only a couple of months back. But there they were. And there was Nick. I was scared to talk to him. I was scared because he was dead. Being dead is scary. Death is scary.

And then I woke up. I was exhausted. I couldn't make heads or tales of what Nick might be trying to tell me. Or what I might be trying to tell Nick. Or what to do with us now that I was thirty-two and a good white person and he was a heap of bones buried in Minneapolis.

I turned over and looked at Katie. I thought for a moment.

At night I had been unstuck. In the morning I was stuck.

At night my dreams traveled. In the morning my writing traveled.

In both spaces I was conjuring some sort of magic. In both spaces, I was trying to run wild.

"Release me," I sang as I drove to work, "release me!"

***

The next night, I found myself dreaming again.

"Mr. Tanner!" Vicky was smiling, "Dinosaurs run wild!"

"Hello, Vicky." I smiled back at her.

"Mr. Tanner, save me!"

I laughed at Vicky.

She laughed with me.

"Mr. Tanner, this place is hell." Vicky was referring to the high school hallway. The fluorescent lights flickered.

I sighed heavily. In a flash of light, Vicky was gone. Nick replaced her. For some reason, Nick and I were glowing. It was as though we had been struck by lightning. Twice.

"Sam," Nick was smoking a cigarette, "you're a jackass."

"Hello, Nick." I smiled at him.

"Want a drag?"

I laughed at Nick. He knew I didn't smoke.

He laughed at me.

"Nick, I think we might be in hell." I was referring to our blank context. The space was still. Nothing moved.

Nick inhaled deeply.

"I got married, Nick, what do you think of that?"

Again, Nick was silent.

"I would have liked for you to have been there."

And Nick smirked mischievously.

"How do you know I wasn't?"

In a flash of light, Nick was gone. Katie replaced him. And Katie was looking at me. She leaned over and kissed me on my forehead.

"Sam," Katie said, "are you okay? You were talking in your sleep."

I looked at the clock. It was three in the morning.

"I'm okay." I pulled Katie closer to me. We held each other tightly in our bedroom.

For some reason, we were glowing.

***

I woke up the next morning and found myself in front of my laptop again. The screen glowed. The high school classroom didn't.

Writing was pouring out of me. This book was sprawling into every part of my life. Nick was being conjured. He had something to say. I had something to say. *We* were trying to speak.

Something was running wild. *Something* was being conjuring. *Something* was happening.

This book kept happening as I kept learning how to travel forward through an enormous, complicated universe. I suppose that is part of a funeral, moving forward.

- C H A P T E R 6 -

Long before Nick did himself in, he and I almost had a bullet put in both of our brains.

When we were sophomores, we used to drive to school in a carpool with our friend Mike. Mike was the first of our group of friends to get his license. His parents gave him their 1980 Cadillac to drive. The year was 1996 so the car was long past its prime.

We tried to convince Mike to get bullhorns to put on the grill. It was nearly identical to the car that Boss Hog drove on the original Dukes of Hazzard.

"Only needs the horns," Mike would always say. And then Nick would tell Mike that he looked like Beau and then I would tell Nick that he looked like Cletus and then Nick would tell me that I looked like Daisy and then we would all laugh like fools.

A great heaping hulk of metal, the entire frame shook when Mike accelerated. This was the car that used to take us to and from school when we were sophomores.

For a brief period of time, we took up bowling after school. A car meant the freedom to go out and do something and bowling was doing something.

I was never much of a bowler. I have really small hands. Our physics teacher in high school once noticed their size.

"You are like a carny, Sam," he announced in front of the whole class. Mike had thought that was hysterical.

Apparently carnys had small hands? I didn't learn much that I remembered from our physics teacher, but I learned that. Public education is a powerful system, right?

Anyways, when we used to bowl, I would use a pink ball and prance my way to and from the stripe. My friends would name me Princess on the scorecard. This was both a reference to the character that I used in the video game *Mario Kart* as well as a jab at my masculinity.

Jerks.

Mike's name on the scorecard was D-Hog. I created the name as an amalgam of his last name, Dougherty, and

70

Snoop's last name, Dawg. John was another friend of ours in the carpool. We named him Mookie. This was a reference to Mookie Blaylock, the point guard for the Atlanta Hawks as well as the original name of Nick's favorite band, Pearl Jam. Nick's name was The Beast. This was a nod to his temper.

Whenever Nick would throw a gutter ball, he would curse, jump up and down, and throw his hat. He acted like a wild animal. This amused us to no end. He would laugh about it too. The Beast.

One time we were bowling in a lane next to a mother and her little daughter. This was the sort of bowling that involved inflatable bumpers so as to avoid gutter balls. Nick went up to his lane to bowl. The little girl went up to her lane to bowl. Nick politely waited for the little girl to finish. She walked up to her lane and heaved the ball directly over the inflatable bumper and into Nick's lane. And because we couldn't figure out the electronic scoring, Nick was credited with a gutter ball. This made us laugh. This made Nick angry.

Later in the same game, Nick tossed his ball into the gutter of his own volition. Out came The Beast. He jumped up and down and threw his Seattle Supersonics baseball hat. The hat tore through the universe and hit the little girl in the face. The little girl started to cry. Her mother was extremely pissed off. I fell out of my chair laughing. So did D-Hog, so did Mookie, and The Beast joined in on the drive home.

Funny stuff.

So one Tuesday afternoon, we went bowling after school.

We finished up around four in the afternoon and Mike was going to drive us home. We got into his Cadillac and he pulled up behind a big black SUV so as to take a right turn onto Highway 10.

I was sitting shotgun. John and Nick were in the backseat. John was drinking a Coke.

We waited for a minute behind the SUV. There was no traffic in sight, yet the SUV was not budging. Mike's road rage started to set it.

"What the hell? Come on!"

We waited another minute, and the SUV was still stationary.

"Just go around it!" This was John.

"Pass the jackass!" This was Nick.

Mike threw the car into reverse in order to pull back and pass the SUV.

"Hey Sam, you should throw my pop on their hood as we pass them!" John said.

"Teach 'em a lesson!" Nick agreed.

It struck us that it would be great comedy if we threw John's pop on the car's windshield. This was probably because we were sophomores in high school.

So John handed me his pop. I rolled the window down. As we drove by, I tossed the pop out the window and it exploded all over the SUV's windshield.

We were howling with laughter as we sped away.

It was at this moment that the SUV finally decided to take their right turn. They took it fast. They were in hot pursuit.

Mike gunned the Caddy. More a tank than a car, it rumbled as it accelerated to top speed. When it got there, it had all the gathered momentum of vintage American steel. So we watched as the SUV fell away into the distance. We were applauding each other with laughter as we came up to the intersection of Highway 10 and Highway 96. It was here that we needed to take a left turn in order to get back to our neighborhood. As Mike pulled up, the left turn arrow turned from yellow to red. So we pulled to a stop.

Sure enough, the SUV exploded over the horizon behind us, glowing with anger. I remember flames of fury as it tore towards us. There were no cars next to us and so the SUV was going to be able to pull up directly next to us. Our laughter turned to anxiety. What would we do?

Sitting shotgun, I was in the most immediate danger. So I came up with a solution. I put my hand up as a blinder to shield the SUV from my face. I started humming to myself.

"Doo-doo-da-de-doo."

So we were staring dumbly forward as the SUV pulled up alongside us. It was then that I felt an energetic transformation in the car. I sensed that something in the car had shifted.

"Sam, roll down the window." Mike's voice was deathly serious.

"Roll down the window, I ain't rolling down the window! Are you crazy? We just threw pop on their car!" I kept my hand raised.

"Sam, roll down the window. She has a gun."

Sure enough, I looked up to see a middle-aged woman in a business suit waving a pistol back and forth at me. She was screaming. She was pissed off. She was as much a Beast as Nick.

I rolled the window down. The most horrible profanity was oozing out of this woman's mouth.

"I'm gonna kill you high-school kids, I'm going to kill you!" She continued on like this.

It seemed to me like she was working herself up to commit a homicide. She seemed intent on putting a bullet in at least one of our brains.

In fact, I remember one thing she said in particular.

"I'm gonna call the cops on you damned high-school kids."

I remember thinking to myself, please, for the love of God, please call the cops. You are waving a pistol at four high-school kids. Get the cops out here!

This woman kept getting angrier and angrier. Finally, thinking it the safer option, Mike floored the Caddy through a red light and into oncoming traffic. We swerved our way through the intersection and traveled to safety.

What is the moral of this story? Don't mess with

people. They might shoot you in the face.

***

Lots of people messed with Nick. He didn't shoot anyone else in the face. He did it to himself instead.

***

Did I say messed with?

At school, Nick was one of the only few kids who wasn't white. He grew up learning that he was different, that he was Asian.

It never seemed to bother him but nothing is ever what it seems, right?

He shrugged off the jokes about his slanty eyes the same way I shrugged off the jokes about my Jewish greed.

In middle school, he and I sat together on the bus. The cool kids smoked pot in the back, the mentally challenged girl sat up front next to the bus driver, and Nick and I sat in between them and complained about the radio station. It was the early 90's and Seal was all the rage. His voiced filled the bus as it took us to school.

"I've been kissed by a rose on the range," I rolled my eyes at Nick.

"You are my pleasure, my power, my pain," Nick mimed singing with great emotional passion.

Then he and I would laugh and talk about Nintendo.

We got straight A's and we were too short to be dangerous on the basketball court. So I guess we were kind of dorky. This made it easy for people to mess with us. The cool kids were too busy scoring with the hot girls to take much notice of us. When they did, we became easy targets. When one of them made fun of me because I was pudgy, Nick would laugh with me about the grammatical inaccuracy of their vernacular assault.

We shrugged off eighth grade and found comfort in

74

making jokes with each other.

Later, I became a high school teacher and Nick blew his brains out.

I spent my adulthood trying to make adolescents be kind to each other. I hate when people mess with each other.

Nick spent his somewhere else.

***

In high school, Nick and I took German together. As freshmen, we signed up with Josh so that we could have a class together. None of us gave a damn about German, but we sure liked being together. We liked making each other laugh. This drove our German teacher crazy. Poor woman.

More often than not, we were in the back of the classroom making jokes about her abusing her children or setting up concentration camps during summer vacation. Most of our humor was in extremely poor taste.

Anyway, one of the few assignments that Nick and I completed in German class was something called spaB punte.

Here I would ask you to forgive my German.

Though I completed four years in high school and the University of Minnesota pronounced me proficient in the language, I am less than convinced that I learned anything.

I recently had a German exchange student in an 11th grade English class. I tried to strike up conversations in her mother tongue at every opportunity. She mostly rolled her eyes and giggled. It was fun for me so I kept doing it.

"Wie geht's es ihnen Fraulein, bitte heute?"

"Mr. Tanner, that is incorrect."

"Ja, ich bin eihne Lehrer, jawohl?"

My student laughed.

I digress.

SpaB punte or "fun points" was one of the only assignments that Nick and I were given in high school that allowed deviation from multiple choice tests and standardization. Our teacher gave us options such as making skits, writing stories, and so on. One of the options for this assignment was filming a video using the German that we had been working on during the semester.

Josh, Nick and I liked being together and making each other laugh so we decided to complete that assignment.

From freshmen year until we were seniors, we filmed nearly thirty hours of footage on Nick's parent's camera. Our work included things like me getting hit by a car, a staged appearance by Charles Manson and his family on the Oprah Winfrey show, and an expose on our German teachers abuse of her children. We spoke in broken German that was mostly English with a couple of "Jawohls!" thrown in for good measure.

Prior to drafting this book, I hadn't seen these videos in nearly ten years. In college, for fun, my friends used to take them out and watch them. Have a couple of beers, invite over some girls from across the hall, and horrify them with our antics, right? Then Nick blew his brains out and his parents wanted the videos back.

After I started drafting this book, reaching out to Nick with a literary expedition into boogie land, his mother emailed and asked if we could all watch the videos together.

How is that for the magic of this project?

Anyway, during our tenth grade year in German, there was a girl that was Mormon in our class. She was cute so we made fun of her for being Mormon. Needless to say, this was not an effective mating ritual. She didn't date any of us. But she would laugh when we made jokes at her expense. I always liked it when people laughed, especially cute girls.

I digress again.

We thought it would be funny to make a German video about Mormons because of this girl in our class. So we thought about the Mormons that we were familiar with.

We came up with Joseph Smith, Brigham Young, and Steve Young, the quarterback of the 49ers at the time.

So we put all of these characters into the game show, *Jeopardy!* I played Alex Trebeck and Josh played Steve Young.

And because one of the only things we knew about Mormons was that they had multiple wives, Nick played one of Steve's multiple wives. In the middle of the game show, Nick peeked his head out from behind Steve's podium. This implied that he had been down there giving Steve oral sex for the duration of the scene. If this wasn't bad enough, we decided to put white frosting on Nick's face. This was meant to simulate Steve's semen as the result of an act of ejaculation. Steve scolded his wife when she appeared from under the podium in our scene. He told her to go back to work.

"Gehen sie zu arbeit, bitte!" Go back to work!

"Jawohl!" Absolutely!

Needless to say, our German teacher was not impressed. Neither was the cute Mormon girl. In fact, our German teacher held us after class. Looking very much like Big Bird, she pointed her finger in our faces.

"Keine punte, keine punte, keine punte! Zero, zero, zero!"

This translated into a grade that Nick and I received more often than not in high school. F.

But I have to admit, even as I wrote this story down, I couldn't help but smile at the silliness of the whole thing. Nick's willingness to go for the cheap laugh still impressed me.

I miss his sense of humor.

***

After Mike first got his license, we were very much excited to go cruisin' the streets of Shoreview. Shoreview was as white of a neighborhood as Arden Hills and near an even whiter neighborhood, North Oaks.

Incidentally, North Oaks was one of the few places in the world that would not appear on Google maps. I guess that rich white people valued their privacy.

So we crammed into Mike's 1980 Cadillac. We included Mike, Josh, Nick, and I.

After an hour of driving around Shoreview, we got bored and ended up at McDonalds. With seventy-four cents to our name, we pooled our money and bought Mike a hamburger. We couldn't afford cheese.

To tell this story, it is important to describe the seating arrangement. I was sitting directly across from Josh. Nick was sitting beside me and Mike was next to Josh.

Bored and frenetic, I was playing with a ketchup packet. I was massaging it, rubbing it on my face, and acting like a jackass.

"Sam," Nick said, "you are acting like a jackass."

Mike grew irritated at my behavior as well. He voiced his irritation furiously.

"Sam, stop playing with the packet."

I continued rubbing it on my face. I started to hum to myself as I did it.

"Sam, you look like an idiot," Mike said again.

I smiled as I played with the packet.

"Sam, you are going to break the packet." Mike tried to make me stop a third time.

And then a miraculous thing happened. I heard a pop. Before a nanosecond could pass, Josh was standing up in the middle of a crowded McDonalds.

"My eye," he screamed, "my eye!"

Josh was clutching his eye with his hands. I thought that it had come clear out of his head. I asked Josh if he was okay. I was worried. Mike and Nick, on the other hand, were laughing like idiots.

As Josh continued screaming and I told Mike to take us to the hospital, Nick nudged my shoulder. I half turned to him. He was slumped over.

"Sam," Nick said.

"What?"

"Sam, get me a napkin."

"A napkin? Why the hell do you want a napkin? Josh's eye is gonna fall out over here and you want me to get you a napkin?"

"Sam, I laughed so hard that I threw up on myself."

Sure enough, Nick had laughed so hard that he had thrown up on himself. I went and got him a napkin. In fact, I got him a handful. There was a lot of puke. Josh went to the bathroom.

When Josh came back from the bathroom, his eye was blood red. We sheepishly walked out of McDonalds as the customers eyed us with embarrassed contempt.

Outside, we examined the packet. Again, it was miraculous. There wasn't a single fluid ounce of ketchup left in the packet. Nor had any sprayed on the table or on Josh's face. Every bit of ketchup had managed to travel across the table and land directly in Josh's eye socket.

Nick took his jacket off and left it in Mike's trunk. Incidentally, Mike's parents found the jacket three months later. It was crusted in moldy puke.

That is one of my favorite stories about Nick. Every time I tell it or think about it, I laugh.

Incidentally, I will point out here that Nick had acid reflux problems. His stomach was always bothering him.

***

As I have written, Nick and I spent a good chunk of our summer after eighth grade with our friend Josh. This usually entailed sleepovers.

One of our houses always became the gathering place. Josh had a computer. That was a draw. I had a neglectful single father who let us get away with anything. That was a draw. Nick had overbearing and caring parents. They fed us well. That was a draw.

We would play video games all night. It was computer games at Josh's house. We mastered games like *Lands of Lore* or *Frontpage Football 94*. It was Nintendo and Super Nintendo at my house or Nick's house. Hours were spent playing *Baseball Stars*, *Final Fantasy*, or *Tecmo Super Bowl*.

We would eat pizza. We would drink Mountain Dew. The room, whatever room, usually smelled like stale death by the morning. It was gross. One morning after one of our sleepovers at Nick's house, Josh was convinced that Nick's dog Yoda had taken a shit somewhere behind the couch. We were all disturbed to discover that Nick's breath was the source of the odor. We were too busy enjoying each other's company to brush our teeth.

One particular sleepover, sometime in the summer, we found ourselves melting in the sweltering heat of Josh's house. That there was no air conditioning was a problem. We would have gone over to my house but, as I have said, Josh had a computer and we were deep into a season on *Frontpage Football*. My Chicago Bears were playing staunch defense with Chris Zurich at nose tackle. Josh's Detroit Lions were running amuck with Barry Sanders. Nick let Warren Moon loose and his Minnesota Vikings had a deadly passing assault. Our NFC Central was far more interesting than the one our underachieving Vikings stumbled through year after year.

Anyway, our solution to the heat was to beg for a couple of bucks from Josh's mom and head down the street to the Tom Thumb convenience store on the corner. For a dollar, you could buy a box of 100 Mr. Freezies. A Mr. Freezie was artificial fruit juice packed into a plastic tube. Once frozen, the Mr. Freezie was a suitable way to imbibe copious amounts of sugar. And we liked them so we picked up two boxes.

It took us most of the night to work our way through 200 Mr. Freezies. My favorite flavor was purple. So was Josh's. We raced through them.

Josh became a vampire. By that I mean that, if he were

too lazy to get up and find a scissors, he could bite into an unfrozen Mr. Freezie from the center and suck every last drop of juice out.

He would leave these two little holes in the center of the plastic tube. Perfect little incisions. I tried to use his technique and ended up with a mouthful of plastic and a face full of sticky fruit-flavored juices. It was gross. Josh and Nick laughed at me. I am sure I laughed too. We were fools.

So we finished off the Mr. Freezies. Sweltering again, we begged for another dollar from Josh's mom and headed back to the Tom Thumb. A pleasant Sunday morning, unshowered and delirious with sugar and a lack of sleep, we ambled down the middle of Josh's street. Nick grabbed his stomach.

"I don't feel so good."

Josh and I looked at each other.

And Nick stopped in the middle of the street. He opened his mouth. Waves of multi-colored vomit spewed forth from his mouth. It was a rainbow of puke.

Once again, we were all laughing like fools.

When he was finished, we asked him if he was going to be all right. He said he was fine. So we bought another 100 Mr. Freezies and finished them off by late afternoon.

Nick's acid reflux be damned, he probably had more than his fair share of the freezies.

***

In high school, Nick never had much luck with the ladies.

For a while, one of our friend's younger sisters started catching rides with our carpool in the morning and after school. This was during our senior year.

And Rebecca was smoking hot.

Nick would usually sit quietly in the backseat while I fumbled through small talk.

Rebecca was sitting shotgun in my 1984, Oldsmobile Cutlass Cierra. I used to describe the car as four cylinders of chick magnet. That description made Nick laughed.

"So, what's up?" I would ask Rebecca.

"Nothing."

"Oh."

"..."

"..."

And while I was anything but a playa, at least I was cordial.

Nick, on the other hand, was silent and enigmatic.

One afternoon, as we were driving home, my 1984 Cutlass began to smell of something most foul. Nick's acid reflux was acting up.

Rebecca and I looked at each other in relative degrees of disgust.

Finally, Nick broke his self-imposed silence.

"I have gas," he said angrily.

Rebecca stopped riding with us soon after that.

Smooth, you son of a bitch, real smooth.

***

Nick had a bad stomach as long as I knew him.

When we were watching the music video for *Smells Like Teen Spirit* by Nirvana, Nick probably had a stomachache.

When we were laughing like fools at Weird Al's *Smells Like Nirvana,* Nick stomach was probably upset.

And after Kurt Cobain put a bullet in his brain, when we were listening to *Pennyroyal Tea* on *Nirvana Unplugged* and playing Final Fantasy III in his parent's basement, Nick was probably popping Rolaids.

Poor guy.

Incidentally, another of our favorite albums when we were thirteen was *Nevermind* by Nirvana. Nick had the same issue with his stomach that Kurt Cobain had with his.

Both Nick and Kurt shot themselves in the head.

Let me give you another example of lightning striking twice.

It turned out that my stepfather Jim had an undiagnosed stomach ailment prior to his suicide. For a year, he had been going to the hospital to find out what was wrong. No luck.

In fact, in the garage, next to where my mother found his body, there was a cardboard box with an elaborate medical device that was meant to test his stomach. He never had a chance to use it. For that matter, he never had a chance to explain to me how the hell it worked. I couldn't make sense of it when I stumbled upon it later.

Eventually, after harassing the hospital with phone calls blaming them for the death of her husband, my mom tossed the contraption into the garbage.

Two days prior to his suicide, Jim had been talking with his sister on the phone about his stomach.

"The pain is so bad," he said, "I'm just going to kill myself."

"Oh Jim," she had laughed, "stop it."

"I'm just kidding," he said.

Two days later, Jim woke up. He shaved off his mustache, told my mother he loved her, and put a bullet in his brain.

That is one way to deal with stomach pain.

- CHAPTER 7 -

Somewhere in that space between spaces, in all that blankness, clouds were gathering. *They* were charging them with electrical energy.

The author Magic "Fucking" Johnson was with Nick now. They were walking along the banks of the River Styx. It was a foggy scene. Nick's only discernable feature was the gaping hole in his head. Magic's smile shone through the haze given off by the river. They were surrounded by lost and menacing souls.

Or something like that.

"You was so caught up on yourself, baby, that you couldn't see nothing else. You was isolated." Magic's voice was laughter.

"What the hell would you know, jackass?" Nick's voice was sarcasm.

"The hell, that is what I would know, baby, the hell." Magic smiled.

Nick laughed.

"You was isolated," Magic continued, "and you are still isolated. You gotta give that up baby. You gotta let yourself become what *they* are." Magic pointed into the distance. Just barely visible, something was glowing somewhere. Nick was struggling to make it out.

"Now that is some bullshit," Nick lit another cigarette.

"No, *that* is some bullshit," Magic pointed at the hole in Nick's head.

Nick's hand drifted up to his face. He pulled it away in surprise at what it found.

"The only way past that, Nick, is to let *them* take you *there*. To let *them* take *us there*."

Nick was trying not to listen to Magic.

"I was stuck by lightning twice, baby, so so were you."

Nick continued to follow Magic as he headed towards the glow in the distance.

"Something isn't right," Nick said.

"Damn straight," Magic smiled.

Nick remembered sitting in his bedroom. He had

loaded the AR-15 assault rifle. He positioned it in his mouth. After that, things got complicated.

Magic was walking calmly. There was no hurry in his purposeful gait.

"Where are we going?" Nick groaned.

"*There*, Nick, we are going *there*. We are going to meet *them*."

"Real specific, you jackass."

Magic laughed loudly. His voice echoed throughout the vacuum.

"That is one of the problems, Nick, your specifics."

Magic stopped walking. Nick lit a cigarette. By blinking his eyes, Magic conjured a basketball court. It was shadowy and vague. He tossed a basketball at Nick. Nick caught it instinctively.

"Good basketball, Nick," Magic said, "is when a team of players stops trying to play for themselves and starts trying to play for each other. The team lets the game go where it has to go. They start to solidify and *their* energy becomes magical, baby."

Nick looked at the basketball. An image of his mother and father came into his mind. He blinked it away.

"Bad basketball," Magic continued, "Is when people are so caught up on their own game that they start to blame their teammates for everything that goes wrong. Bad basketball is when people have their own idea about what it means for things to go wrong. Bad basketball is when the players don't open their conceptions of what should or shouldn't happen to the fluid ebb and flow of what the game allows. Bad basketball is when people get too caught up on their own specifics."

Though he tried to shut Magic out, Nick couldn't help but to listen. Magic's voice was piercing.

"And good basketball is good living, Nick. It is when we do *this* together." Magic took a moment to refer to the inordinate complexities of cells and organisms working together. At least, this is what Nick saw in Magic's eyes as his smile seemed to conjure a note from a flute.

"It is the opposite of that, Nick."

Magic nodded to the gaping hole in Nick's head.

"*They* taught me how to play the right way, Nick and so I'm gonna show you too, baby."

Magic was referring to the twelve beings of inordinate light that he met after that second bolt of lightning struck him in the head.

"*They* taught me that it is going to be okay, Nick."

Magic grabbed Nick's hands. Magic smiled. He blinked his eyes. He motioned to Nick to blink with him. At first Nick was resistant. But Magic was persistent. Bewildered, Nick acquiesced. And Magic and Nick blinked their eyes together.

Nick felt electricity shoot through him. It was as though he had been struck by lightning. The thunderheads above them rang out.

The basketball court disappeared. Magic and Nick were now standing on a dock. A wooden boat was moored on the River Styx. The boat gave off a glow. Inside the boat sat a figure of no real shape or definition. Nick vaguely recognized the traveler.

"For an improbable world," Magic told Nick, "you need a special vehicle."

Inside of that boat, Sam was typing away in front of his glowing laptop.

"For an improbable world," Sam wrote in his book about his friend Nick, "you need a special vehicle."

Sam looked up and saw two shapes standing on a dock. He vaguely recognized both of them.

Magic led Nick into the boat. He untied the rope from the dock and the boat started to drift into the still water.

Clouds continued to form overhead as the three figures set out on an improbable journey across the River Styx.

Or something like that.

***

Sam's writing was a vehicle that allowed him to travel to his friend Nick. This traveling led him to a space between spaces. In all that blankness, he found himself in a boat with the author Magic "Fucking" Johnson and his friend Nick. They appeared to be drifting on the River Styx.

Okay.

"Nick?" Sam asked.

"Sam?" Nick asked.

Silence echoed throughout the vacuum.

Nick took out a pack of cigarettes and a lighter that he had received as a birthday present from his father. Sam thought about what to say. He put his laptop aside and took hold of an oar. He looked towards Magic. Magic smiled and watched them silently. Sam started to row.

"Nick," Sam tried to make conversation as he rowed, "have I told you that I am working on my PhD?"

His voice boomed across the vacuum as though it were a burst of thunder.

"Ain't you something special, Sam? Always on your high horse."

Nick recognized Sam for a moment. He laughed. So did Sam. Sam continued.

"Right now, I am sitting pretty at a 4.0."

"You had a 2.1 in high-school and you have a 4.0 in graduate school?"

"Damn straight."

Nick smirked. He lit another cigarette. He took a drag. His face composed itself. Nick was stoic again.

Sam took notice of the gaping hole in Nick's head.

"Nick," Sam said, "what do I have to do to cheer you up?"

"What the hell does that mean?"

"It means that I want you to be happy."

"No you don't. You just want to make yourself happy."

Sam paused and thought.

"Is it so wrong that making you happy would make me happy?"

Now Nick paused and thought.

"You are a jackass."

Sam turned to Magic.

"Magic," Sam said, "what do I do?"

"Sam, you don't have to do nuthin'. Just shut up and let the universe sing, will ya?" Magic said.

Nick and Sam were silent. Magic started whistling. But it wasn't Earvin Johnson making the music. It was the universe. It almost sounded like the song *Release Me* by the band Pearl Jam. The music was coming through Magic. This music is what *they* had taught him. It was the reason he had since become the author of *I Was Struck By Lightning Twice, So So Were You!*, Magic "Fucking" Johnson.

The boat glided easily through the still water. The three travelers were moving now. Sam turned back to Nick.

"You know, it would have been nice to have had you around these past ten years."

Nick didn't say anything.

"You are my friend, you know?"

Nick blew out a perfectly formed smoke ring. It drifted upwards.

Clouds continued to form overhead. The River Styx was dead still. Something was about to happen but Sam and Nick weren't quite sure what.

Sam continued to paddle. Nick smoked. Magic smiled.

"Nick," Sam said, "I am trying to write a book about you, about *us*."

Nick took a drag off of a cigarette. He exhaled another perfectly formed smoke ring and regarded Sam coolly.

"Do you remember the book you wrote about me?"

Nick's eyes registered the memory and his lips twisted into an almost indiscernible smile.

"Creative writing class?"

"Yes."

"I don't remember the story. I don't know if I ever

read the whole thing. But you wrote hundreds of pages."

Nick laughed as he remembered.

Sam continued. "I wonder if your parents still have the story somewhere, I would love to read it. Do you think that they kept it?"

Nick paused as though he were remembering something.

"I would love to read that story now." Sam grew thoughtful.

After a moment of silence, Sam continued speaking. "You know, when I had dinner with your mom and dad last summer, I was excited to see Willy and Yoda. But they are dead now. They had just put Willy down and Yoda had been gone for a couple of years."

"Willy and Yoda are dead?"

"At your funeral, your dad gave all of your friends little porcelain figures of Willy as remembrance of you. And one of the only positive things that the priest could think of to say about you at the funeral was that you loved those dogs."

Nick was silent.

"The only thing I could think to say was that I had so many stories I could share about you, but that none of them were appropriate for the occasion. The funeral was too solemn and formal. I didn't want to share you there. I didn't figure you would have wanted me to either."

Nick and Sam made eye contact.

"Anyway, I am trying to write a book about that. Actually, I think that it is about *this*." Sam referred to the universe around them.

"Well good luck." Nick took another drag and exhaled another perfectly formed smoke ring.

Time passed. Nothing happened. The journey seemed to stretch out in all directions at once. The boat was both moving and staying still.

Nick and Sam were silent. Magic began to speak. His voice was something like music.

"Can you see *it*?" He said. "Can you hear *it*?"

"What?" Sam asked.

Nick took a deep drag. Magic opened his eyes wide and began to speak. His words harmonized.

"You just gotta let yourself open up, baby, and you can see it all around you. Ain't nuthin' more perfect than when *we* get lost in the magic of *this* song. Our words are the notes. The problem is that we say 'em all jumbled up together. Everybody is so busy trying to talk, that nobody listens. But when we figure out how to say 'em in a rhythm, like good basketball, we start to transform. We start to sing a new song. And we become what we should be. We become infinite energy. We become expanding consciousness. We gain momentum and then we start traveling, baby. Ain't nowhere we can't go and ain't nuthin' we can't do. But we gotta let ourselves get *there*, baby. And we gotta stop pretending that we know where *there* is or what *there* looks like. You are so frightened. That is why I am here. I can teach you to be less afraid. That is all I can do. You gotta stop acting like you know how to travel so that you can start *traveling*. You gotta listen with *this*," Magic referred to the expanse around them, "instead of this" he pointed to his head.

Nick looked off into the distance. He thought he saw something glowing. He wasn't sure what.

Sam thought about what Magic had said.

Magic's laughter echoed like lightning through that space between spaces.

After awhile, Sam tried small talk again.

"Nick," Sam said, "I am married now."

"Ain't that something?" Nick coughed sarcastically.

"Your parents were there."

"So? What's your point?"

"I don't know."

"Huh."

"I guess it would have been nice if you were there. You would have been the best man. It was Mike and Josh

91

instead. They did it together."

At the names Mike and Josh, Nick seemed to remember something else. He took a drag of his cigarette.

A storm was building energy in the distance. Soon Nick and Sam would be different. For now, they were traveling.

"Maybe I could rescue you, Nick?" Sam thought aloud, "maybe I could bring you back?"

"Always on your high horse, Sam?"

"Maybe I could save you, Nick?"

"From what?"

"From this." Sam spread his arms out and referred to the tumult of the river Styx beneath the boat that was containing Sam and Nick's conversation.

Nick blew a perfectly formed smoke ring.

"Don't be a jackass, Sam. I chose to come here."

"You like it here?"

Nick blew another perfectly formed smoke ring. It caught up with the first ring, combined with it, and created an even more perfect formation of smoke.

Nick lit another cigarette. Sam struggled blindly with a paddle. The sky grew darker as a gust of wind rocked the boat back and froth. Chaos reverberated through the universe.

A great storm was coming.

Magic sat back in the boat and waited for *it* to happen.

- C H A P T E R 8 -

Mrs. Wiseman came over to watch the German videos with Josh and I after my wedding. Mr. Wiseman was planning on joining us but, at the last minute, he decided that it would be too much for him.

Mrs. Wiseman brought bottles of white and red wine. She also brought cards for Josh and I that told us how important we were to her and Pete. The cards began by reminding us that it was the tenth anniversary of Nick's death.

After making small talk and munching on food, I popped the video in. I had made copies of them on DVD.

Josh and I had been talking about doing this for years. Finally, I got my hands on a device that transferred VHS to DVD from my high school. Mrs. Wiseman gave us the first of two videos and I made copies.

She sat next to me on the couch in my living room. She had a box of Kleenex and a glass of wine. Katie sat next to me. Josh was on the edge of the couch.

We watched. Josh and I laughed as we translated our broken German. Katie rolled her eyes when she saw my buckteeth, my double chin, and my long, wavy hair. I had changed a great deal since I was fourteen.

Josh and I laughed like fools when Nick came on screen as Mr. T. We had shaved his head so that he had a Mr. T. Mohawk. We did this as we reenacted Rocky Three. I played Rocky. Josh played Rocky's trainer, Mic. Nick was the villain. We used Mike Tyson's punch-out for Nintendo to recreate the boxing matches. This required Josh to play all the way through the game so that we could fight Mike Tyson. The computer was no match for Josh's lightning thumbs. Nick wore that haircut to school the next day. What a badass.

Mrs. Wiseman laughed through her tears as the videos played out.

In another segment, I came out in my boxer shorts.

"Haben gern do meine body?" Do you like my body?

This was a parody of a Calvin Klein commercial that

objectified young models. In another clip, Nick put Mickey Mouse ears on and played our German's teacher's son. He showed up on the Oprah Winfrey Show and complained that his mother beat him. Oprah invited his mother to come out. A picture of our German teacher that we swiped from her desk played this character. Later during that same show, I came out as Charles Manson and did a rendition of an original song entitled "Frauen Sind Dumm." Women Are Dumb.

Incidentally, the only censorship our teacher imposed came when she asked me to cover up the swastika on my forehead.

The second verse of "Frauen Sind Dumm" was "Scharwze Sind Dumm." So I was on camera as a parody of Charles Manson, in front of the entire German class, singing the lines, "women are dumb" and "blackies are dumb." Talk about offensive! Living in that all-white, rich neighborhood must have done something to me. Seventeen years later, I couldn't believe that our teacher let us show those clips. To our credit, Oprah got so angry in the skit that she karate fought the Manson family, played by Nick, to teach them a lesson in diversity and equity.

My favorite part about that skit was that Oprah, played by Josh, changed from fat to skinny in every scene. It was hysterical. We used a pillow.

And it went on like that. We had dozens of skits that we recorded. It took Mrs. Wiseman one year to give us the first volume.

She left abruptly after watching the videos. She started to tell us about a trip she took to Korea after Nick's suicide. This was when we were finished watching the videos. Then, in a matter of moments, she excused herself and was gone.

After she left, Josh and I schemed about how to get the rest of the videos.

***

Prior to his suicide, Nick was going to return to Korea with his mother. They had purchased plane tickets and were planning on leaving the week after her birthday. She had picked him up in Korea from an orphanage. They would start there and explore Nick's geographical home.

A week before they would have left, Nick killed himself in his bedroom.

Talk about a birthday present.

Nick's mom went to Korea about six years later by herself.

After watching the German videos with Josh and me, she sent me an email and asked if I wanted to meet her for lunch.

How could I say no?

We met at a Thai restaurant in Northeast Minneapolis. This is where Katie and I had held our quiet, intimate wedding reception.

"What a wonderful wedding, Sam," Daphne told me when she showed up for lunch.

She showed me pictures from the trip and even shared her journal with me. In her journal, four to five pages, Nick's name was only mentioned once. Perhaps part of the way she continued to survive Nick's suicide was by keeping his presence compartmentalized. This would explain why it took her ten years to sit down and watch the German Videos.

When Nick's mom was explaining her trip to me, she focused on two things.

One, there was a woman in Seoul who lived across the street from Nick's orphanage. When Nick's mom and her accompanying tourists (all families that had been brought together through an adoption agency and this particular orphanage) came to the building, the woman stood on that corner and angrily eyed the Americans and their Korean children.

Nick's mom told me later, at lunch, that she would

have killed to find out what the woman knew.

Though she didn't say it and maybe didn't even think it, I had the inkling that she thought she might have found Nick's biological mother. And I think Daphne was harboring great guilt for what Nick had done.

Two, she spoke about the possibility that Nick had siblings. She so badly wanted to talk to them and apologize for what she and her husband had done. Furthermore, she wanted to touch somebody who had been related to Nick, to hug them.

As she told me these two things, my eyes got weepy. I consoled her the best that I could.

As she got up to leave, I gave her a big hug.

***

The day of Nick's funeral, Nick's mom came up to me and reminded me that, earlier that year, I told her not to worry about Nick.

She had come over to my dad's house in those affluent suburbs about a year before the suicide. She wanted to talk about Nick.

I came upstairs from my basement where I was listening to Peter Gabriel or playing John Madden Football or avoiding my homework from college at all costs. We talked in the foyer of Dad's house, underneath the loft where Nick and I spent our adolescence.

She told me that she was worried about her son.

"His favorite song is *Suicide is Painless*, the theme song from M.A.S.H.," she told me.

"Don't worry, Daphne," I said, "Nick is way to smart for that. He jokes about it but he would never kill himself."

Then Nick put a bullet in his brain.

She reminded me of her visit at Nick's funeral.

I didn't know what to tell her.

***

So after the wedding, after watching the German Videos with Josh and Daphne, and after having lunch with her, it seemed to me that Mr. Wiseman and Mrs. Wiseman couldn't talk about Nick. They were in limbo. Whether it was hiding from footage they have of him, clutching onto his possessions, or changing the subject to the weather, they seemed to do what I did when a woman was pointing a gun at my face in high school. They put their hand up as blinders to shield themselves from pain and hum "Doo-doo-da-de-doo."

And because I cared about them deeply, this troubled me.

So I reached out to my friend Tricia to see if she would have a drink with me and talk.

Like me, Tricia was in her thirties. She was working at the University of Minnesota and had been close friends with Nick. She also cared about Nick's parents a great deal. Tricia had stayed close with Mr. and Mrs. Wiseman after Nick's suicide.

Tricia was also adopted from Korea. White, American Midwesterners also raised her. She was close with Nick because I introduced the two of them when they were sixteen.

Tricia and I worked together at McDonalds when I was fifteen. I convinced Nick to get a job there too. So Nick, Tricia, and I became mutual friends. Tricia and Nick remained close until his suicide. She is probably one of the last people he talked to.

"We had a fight," she told me over drinks, "that was the last time we talked. I always regretted that."

They always had a platonic sort of relationship though it seemed to Josh and Mike that they were perfectly suited for each other.

"I mean they're both Asian, right?" Josh would joke.

When we were sixteen, Tricia and I once bought a bag

of pot while we were closing at McDonalds. I was the manager, so we conducted the deal in the office. One of her friends arrived and we transferred some weed into a little bag. We smoked out in the parking lot and then giggled our way into Perkins where we ate as much as we could.

At the time, McDonalds was using Barbie dolls in their happy meals. I had a crush on Dutch Barbie so we brought her along. She sat next to me in the booth and came very close to getting us kicked out of Perkins.

So it made sense that, as adults, we met for a drink on campus. She was a program director on campus and I was working away at my PhD.

As teenagers, she once told me that she could see me as the kind of guy who would have a beer after work. Having since become that kind of guy, I met Tricia in a bar after teaching high school all day. We got to talking about Nick and Nick's parents.

And I told Tricia that Mike, Josh, and I rarely talked about Nick. I told her that we hadn't really done so after the suicide. I shared the story of how we had sat in the living room for five hours in complete silence on the day that Nick did himself in.

"That is so weird, Sam," she told me.

"Is it?" I asked.

Tricia told me how she had stayed close with Mr. and Mrs. Wiseman long after Nick's suicide. She shared with me that Nick had been writing a great deal before his suicide. She told me that his parents had hundreds of pages of his journals.

As adolescents, Nick and I often talked about being writers when we were older. He wanted to be Frank Herbert or Robert Heinlein. I wanted to be Stephen King or C.S. Lewis.

"What I wouldn't give to see that writing," I told Tricia.

I shared with Tricia that at my wedding, Mr. Wiseman looked to me as though Nick's suicide had killed him. Not physically, but emotionally.

I went on to share that Mrs. Wiseman said something about an emotional death when I met her for lunch after watching the German videos.

"Unlike her husband," I told Tricia, "she was willing to talk about Nick, to a certain extent."

"Pete is so sensitive," Tricia had told me.

"As Daphne and I talked over lunch, I used the word survive to describe what they were doing. She told me that she didn't know that she would call it that. Daphne was referring to the last ten years of her life."

"Wow, Sam."

"I know, right?" I sipped at a Bloody Mary.

The bar was quiet as Tricia and I drank.

"I just care about them so much," I told Tricia. "They were like parents to me, you know?"

"You need to tell them that, Sam."

"I know. I just don't know how."

I paid for the drinks and we went our separate ways. It was the first time we had seen each other or talked about Nick in years.

Walking away, I thought about how much pain there was in Mr. and Mrs. Wiseman when I saw them at my wedding. I suppose there was pain in me as well.

I wanted to be able to tell Mr. and Mrs. Wiseman that it was going to be okay. But I wanted to mean it.

So Magic "Fucking" Johnson showed up as a lubricant and I started to conduct this funeral rite.

This literary ceremony became even stranger than my Judeo-Christian hybrid of a wedding. Part of the reason why I created this book was to try to help Mr. and Mrs. Wiseman get *there*. Sitting across from Daphne at lunch or sitting next to her on the couch or even giving her a hug as she left lunch, it felt like something needed to happen. Only I wasn't sure what *it* was.

It needed to happen for her. It needed to happen for Nick. It needed to happen for me.

It needed to happen for *us*.

***

A couple of months after having lunch with me, Daphne reached out to Josh and I again. She had found another collection of German videos.

"I think Pete might be ready to join us," she told us, "I think it would be good for him."

Josh agreed to host at his house this time.

We set up the event over email. Daphne sent me a note and asked if I would like some of Nick's writing from high school. How could I say no?

I told Josh about Daphne's offer when Katie and I showed up at his posh new house out in the suburbs. By his thirties, Josh was working as an actuary. His math skills and decision to participate in society led to great financial success. Nick had equally impressive math skills as an adolescent. He did not, however, share Josh's willingness to participate in society. Note the bullet.

Anyway, Josh's two daughters were making a great deal of racket as he poured a tall gin and tonic for both him and I.

Nick loved gin and tonics. I suppose Josh was conducting his own sort of memorial for Nick that night as he mixed our drinks.

"Exciting, right?" He was referring to Nick's writing. He figured it would be helpful to my own writing project.

We were waiting for Daphne to show up in his kitchen. We were taking bets on whether or not Nick's dad, Pete, would show up to watch the videos. He had skipped our first viewing session as well as Mike's wedding. Daphne told us it was too painful for him to see Nick's friends. I responded to Josh's question.

"What I really want are the journals that he kept before his suicide. Tricia told me that he had made a chart where he kept track of who was a real person and who was a

101

fake."

Tricia had been Nick's closest friend in the weeks before his suicide.

"What a strange, platonic relationship, right?" Josh was referring to Tricia and Nick.

I laughed.

"You want to see where you are on the list?" Josh laughed. He handed me my gin and tonic.

"That. I'd also like to see where his head was at."

"Before he blew it off?"

I laughed. Josh had never lost his sense of humor.

Daphne showed up without Pete. And she was so nervous that she had gone up to the wrong house. Then she broke two of Josh's wine glasses before the night was over. But we watched the second set of German videos.

In this collection, we were a little older. Braces were straightening my crooked teeth, I was skinnier, I cut my hair, and Josh was over six foot tall.

In the videos, we proceeded to recreate the made for TV special, *I Know my First Name is Steven.*

In the movie, a boy is abducted by a child molester and spends ten years living as his son. Josh played the molester. I was his son. It was terrifying satire.

"Ich verstehe my erste name is Larz," I told the camera. I understand my first name is Larz. Larz was my German name. This was in homage to Lars Ulrich, the drummer for the band Metallica.

In another segment, we created a scene in a restaurant to display the vocabulary we had been learning in class. I came on screen with a crooked hat, baggy pants, and a cocky attitude. Nick came on with a helmet and a duck. We proceeded to reenact a gangster picking up a retarded person, taking him to dinner, and trying to get some action.

"Mogen see ein bischen hankey pankey?" I asked. Do you want to make some hanky panky? I winked at the camera. Again, terrifying.

Anyways, after Mrs. Wiseman left, Josh said this.

"She was more distant this time, wasn't she?"

She was. She had cried the last time. This time, she seemed distracted by Josh's two little girls. She held the baby instead of looking at the screen. The last time, we had watched them at my house. There were no children there, only two cantankerous cats.

Daphne left me with some of Nick's writing from high school. She also gave me his copy of the soundtrack to the movie Fight Club.

Sadly, Ms. Wiseman's package did not contain Nick's journals he had kept before his suicide.

Lord only knows what has since become of that chapter of Nick's writing.

Incidentally, Nick's favorite movie was Fight Club. So on the way home, I listened to the soundtrack. I searched for the song by the Pixies. At the end of the film, the city explodes and the Pixies provide accompaniment. It is beautiful. Instead of the Pixies, I found Tyler Durden's monologue.

The main character, Durden spends the movie and the book that it is based on delivering social critique. After savaging the social conventions of fine, upstanding people like the people Nick and I went to school with in that nice, white neighborhood, Tyler comes to a phrase.

"You have to give up." Over and over again Tyler repeats this mantra.

As I drove home from Josh's house, I found myself agreeing with Tyler. To me, this freed me up to make my own social conventions. And I found myself wondering what Nick made of Tyler's mantra?

You have to give up.

A funny thought came to me, then. I didn't want Mr. and Mrs. Wiseman to put a bullet in their brains but I *did* want them to give up holding onto their guilt. I wanted them to release Nick.

- CHAPTER 9 -

After Mrs. Wiseman left that Thursday night that we first watched the German videos, Josh stayed and talked with me a bit.

We talked about how weird it was that she shared that she often ran into people who look like Nick and approached them. She tells them that they remind her of her son. She just wants to look at them.

"Didn't you want to make the joke," Josh had said right after Daphne left, "that they all looked alike?"

He was referring to the number of Asian people that Mr. and Mrs. Wiseman might run into that looked like Nick.

It was an awful joke but Katie and I laughed anyway. That is one of the things that Nick, Josh and I shared, an awful and inappropriate sense of humor.

Yes and that night she had told us that Pete had the same experience two weeks back in a nightclub in Northeast Minneapolis. He saw somebody who looked like Nick and put his hand over his mouth, horrified. Daphne told us that best symbolized how Pete had dealt with Nick's suicide.

Then Daphne told us that she was worried that Pete was going to kill himself because he had been depressed lately. They were both retired and had little to do but to pass the time. But she was happy because she had finally convinced him to go talk to somebody about Nick.

She used to try to convince Nick to go to a psychologist. When she succeeded, Nick sat in complete silence for an hour. He wouldn't say a word. Seventeen years later, I was still impressed and astounded by his determination.

I was also impressed with hers. She wanted so badly for her husband to live. She wanted so badly for Nick to have lived as well.

Josh and I kept talking and we remembered that he once got into a fight with Nick in 9th grade keyboarding class. Though they couldn't remember what it was about, they didn't talk to each other for four months. We called them both "black whisper." I don't remember why. I think it had to do with their stubbornness. Black whisper seemed like a name for a horse. Horses were stubborn. So black whisper. Regardless, their commitment to not be the first one to talk to each other was remarkable. They sat next to each other in class, they hung out with each other in our group of friends constantly, and they wouldn't say a word. Finally, Nick sent Josh a postcard from Mexico when he was on a vacation that read, "I am the ultimate black whisper." Then they started talking again as though nothing had happened. Josh told me that he still had that postcard.

That night, Josh and I talked about the email that Mrs. Wiseman sent us prior to our viewing of the first video. In the note, she asked Josh and I if we wanted Nick's *Fight Club* CD. Josh pointed out that this was the first item out of Nick's collection of things that she had ever offered us and, even though we had told her that we wanted it, she didn't bring it. He was convinced that all of Nick's stuff was still in his bedroom downstairs. Ten years later and Mr. and Mrs. Wiseman were still living in that same house and still hoarding all of Nick's stuff.

And Josh and I kept talking. He hadn't been able to attend the one-act that I had just written about Nick. A friend of mine had staged it in his community theatre program. Josh was angry with me for not telling him about it earlier. I told him that I was afraid that it was going to be embarrassingly bad.

It wasn't. It was actually pretty good. Katie cried as she watched the actor that played me hand Nick the gun in the final moment of the show.

I told Josh I wanted to extend the one-act into a longer show. I told him that I thought the first act could be the dinner party that we had with the Wisemans' the previous summer. I wanted to introduce them and the way that they hadn't seemed to progress since Nick's death.

After talking to my friend that directed the one-act, I thought I wanted Nick to be there, mysteriously hovering around the edges of the play. That is what it felt like at that dinner party. There was a picture of him on the mantle, a copy of a story he wrote in third grade, and his ghost was everywhere. But we only mentioned him twice during the dinner. So I wanted him there in the first act of the play.

I figured the second act could be the one-act play I wrote. It was a poker game staged like a funeral. It was set in Nick's parent's basement. Nick was written like he had been showing up in my dreams. He was both there and not there, alive and dead, in a space between spaces.

I told Josh that I didn't know what I wanted the third act to be. After talking for about an hour, he told me it should be all the unanswerable questions about Nick, his suicide, his parents and their subsequent survival or lack thereof.

That seemed right to me.

I never finished that play. Instead, I wrote this book. This became my third act, as it were. I let my drafting take me where it took me.

Josh told me that the last time he talked to Nick, two weeks prior to the suicide, Nick had told him he was never shaving again. They were sitting in a bar on the campus of the University of Minnesota. Josh was finishing his degree in math and Nick was going nowhere. Josh thought this was a weird thing to say at the time. Josh went on to tell me that Nick probably hadn't shaved again before he shot himself.

This reminded me of Jim. I told Josh about my stepdad, Jim. In that pain-medicated haze Mom had lived in for years, she remembered that prior to going outside and putting a bullet in his brain, Jim had shaved his mustache for the first time in twenty years. My mom kissed him before he went to the garage and told him how wonderful he looked. She had been begging him to shave for years. This memory came to my mom after we brought her to a hospital in Hudson on the day of Jim's suicide. She started weeping after she shared it.

"I want to die, Sam, I want to die," she had told me.

"It will be okay, Mom," I had told her. I was holding her hand. "I have been through this before with my friend Nick. It will be hard, but it will be okay."

Josh had thought that Jim hung himself. I told him that Jim used a pistol. I told him that my mom hadn't heard the shot because she was doped up. I told him how she crawled into the garage. She had to crawl because she had recently replaced her second hip. Even though she was only sixty-two at the time, her body was falling apart.

She found Jim on the floor of the garage and tried to give him mouth-to-mouth. It took her ten minutes to realize there was a hole in his head. By the time I got there at 9:00 in the morning, she was drenched in his blood. She was covered in blood until we left her at a psychiatric ward hundreds of miles away in the Wisconsin countryside because that was the only place that would admit her.

"We can't take her in," my Aunt and I told the doctors, "We don't know how to take care of her."

I told Josh that leaving Mom there that night was one of the saddest things I have ever done.

That was the most Josh and I ever talked about Nick and his suicide. It was also the most I had told anybody about Jim and his suicide.

Josh left and Katie and I cleaned up the wine glasses and plates. We watched *Its Always Sunny in Philadelphia.* Had he not put a bullet in his brain, Nick would have liked that show.

People tell me that I look and act a great deal like the character, Charlie. Nick would have laughed like a fool about that.

As if on cue, I dreamed about Nick that night. He was in a different house with different parents. These parents had also adopted him just like Mr. and Mrs. Wiseman. He and I played Frontpage Pro Football on his computer.

That is about all I remember about the dream other than the distinct feeling that Nick, even though he had killed himself, was not gone. He was hovering around the edges, as it were.

Not knowing what else to do, I woke up the next morning, drove to school, and wrote.

***

That weekend, after first watching the German videos with Josh, Mrs. Wiseman, and Katie, I had breakfast with my good friend Mike. He had watched the play that I wrote about Nick. Mike had a couple of ideas about what I should do with the play. So we met at a breakfast place in Northeast Minneapolis. That was where both he and I lived.

Mike sat down and ordered a cup of coffee.

"Really? You had the skinny, dorky redhead kid play me in the play?"

I laughed. The actor that played Mike had been an eighteen year old that fit Mike's description.

We used to make fun of Mike for being a ginger in high school.

"I didn't cast it," I laughed at him, "pure coincidence."

We ordered breakfast. For the first time in years, we started talking about Nick.

Mike told me about the time Nick shared a six-pack of Dos Equis with him on a drive out to Wisconsin.

"We were eighteen," he said, "so it was a pretty big deal to share a beer with a friend. I kept asking him if I could have another and he kept saying yes. He let me drink all of those beers on the drive out. It didn't even bother him."

Though Mike had since become a recovering alcoholic, he smiled as he remembered Nick's generosity. He said something to that affect at Nick's funeral. He talked about how Nick would share whatever he had with whomever he was with, even if it meant he didn't get to drink any of the beers in the six-pack.

I told Mike that I remembered Nick's rage when it came to driving. When Nick was crossing the street, he would walk right into the wake of a traveling car to point out to the driver that they were not moving fast enough. When driving, if a car was braking or moving too slowly in front of him, he would rage and drive ahead to cut the car off. All of this just to point out a person's stupidity.

"He would also say that he was teaching people a lesson," I told Mike.

"I used to say that too," Mike paused and thought for a moment. "I guess I learned that you can't live your life that way. Being angry with stupid people. You have to calm down and figure out how to not let it get to you."

I smiled. I learned that lesson early on because I had to deal with my mom and dad. Nick never learned that lesson.

"You should put that story about Nick sharing his beer with me in your play," Mike told me.

I told Mike that I wanted to expand my one-act about Nick into a full-length play. He thought that the best way to end the play about Nick would be to have him smoking a cigarette on a porch in the middle of nowhere. He would take an irritated puff and say, "we always figured I would end up here. I wouldn't want it any other way."

Mike's idea reminded me that we used to call Nick "grandpa" because he was often angry and stubborn like an old man. Our joke was that he would live until he was 100 and hate every second of it.

Incidentally, they called me "grandma" because I was usually in bed before ten.

Yes and we talked about the music that Nick's dad chose to play at Nick's funeral. He went through Nick's collection and chose two songs. Mike couldn't remember what they were. He figured one had to be a Pearl Jam song because Nick loved Pearl Jam. Mike thought it would be awkward to ask Nick's parents. He was probably right, but

I couldn't remember either and I wanted to know.

"Was "Release Me" one of the songs?" I asked Mike.

"I don't remember."

Mike picked up the bill and we went our separate ways.

After I got home, the phone rang. It was Mike. As he was driving away, he told me that three songs had come on the radio. The first was "You've Got a Friend in Me" by James Taylor. The second was "I Won't Give Up on Us," by Jason Mraz. The final song was "I Shall Be Released" covered by Wilco and the Fleet Foxes.

"I wasn't going to call you, but I had to," he said. "If you were making a movie about what we just talked about, these are the three songs you would play."

I laughed and told him that I understood.

"That is the universe for you," I said.

***

I had a friend at work named Angus Poulin. He also taught English. We shared a frenetic energy. He and I could talk for hours about the trials and tribulations of working and living in a public school. His wild, blue eyes burned as brightly as mine.

During our prep periods or before school, we could go on and on about the complexities of an enormous, complicated universe. He was a couple of years older than me and, in many ways, became a mentor as I lived through my late twenties into my early thirties. Like my friends Mike and Josh, Angus read one of the early drafts of this book.

"It is good," he told me, "but it isn't finished yet."

One morning after I shared a draft of this book, Angus and I got to talking about one of our favorite subjects, the universe. He had great knowledge of non-western systems of spirituality or reality.

"I finally saw a Hmong Shaman, Sam." He wore a goofy grin and paced back and forth as I sat in a desk in

111

his classroom.

We had a Hmong population in our school and he had always wanted to find a way to meet a Hmong Shaman in the Twin Cities. Having finally done so through a former student, he shared his story.

"After talking for two hours, she performed a ritual. My mother came to speak through her."

Angus' real mom had died when he was born. He was talking about his stepmom, a troubled woman who had survived Angus' dad by about a year before passing away.

"The Shaman told me that she wasn't in a good place in the afterlife. So the shaman conducted a ritual to help her. She built a kind of home for my mom in the afterlife. My mom came through the shaman and thanked me."

"Did you believe it was real?" I asked him.

"When the Shaman was speaking, she was saying things that only my mom would have known."

I started to talk to Angus about my book. I told him that it felt like Magic "Fucking" Johnson was a way for me to connect to Nick in the afterlife.

"Being struck by lightning is a shamanic trait," he told me. "Magic is like a psychopomp. A psychopomp is a guide whose primary function is to escort souls to the afterlife. They can also serve as guides through the various transitions of life."

I laughed because our conversation was so out there. They usually were. He continued talking as he paced around his room with a spastic sort of energy that seemed to run wild to me.

"Maybe you have already thought of this, but the song *Release Me* reminds me of the release of a basketball, a cosmic golden ball traveling through space toward its destination, its source home. Your writing is illuminating Nick's soul as it is being released as a cosmic basketball with the aid of the psychopomp, Magic Johnson."

I laughed again. That sounded about right to me.

"If you want to see this shaman about Nick, Sam, let

me know."

I didn't know if I wanted to see a shaman. Instead, I kept writing this book.

***

Last night I came awake as though a bolt of lightning had struck me.

I had been dreaming about Nick and Nick's dad. As always, the specifics were vague.

When I awoke, I felt as though Nick were in the room. It felt like he wanted something from me.

Afraid, I buried myself under the covers.

"Go away," I thought, "I can't help you."

Lying there in bed, I thought about what Angus had said about the Hmong shaman. Maybe Nick needed help being released?

Struggling to fall asleep, I remembered that not long after Jim had committed suicide, I woke up in the same way and felt as though Jim were in the room.

"There is nothing I can do, Jim," I had thought to myself, "just go about your way."

And whether or not Jim and Nick were in the room with me, it sure felt as though they were.

I wrote as much the following morning.

***

Later, after spending the morning writing in my classroom, I stumbled back up to Angus' classroom to talk.

"I just remembered something sitting here and talking with you, Sam," He told me. "I think I felt your Asian friend that committed suicide the other night."

If anybody was sensitive to the spirit realm, it was Angus.

"You felt Nick?"

"During a dream, I felt him come to me. I felt a strong, sensitive spirit. He felt wounded."

And I felt a shiver run wild up and down my spine. His description conjured Nick in my mind.

"It just felt like your writing was really important, like he still had something to say and your writing was a way for him to say it."

I laughed. Then I was silent.

"He was such a strong presence," Angus said.

"Yes," I said, "he was."

***

Later, after writing about what Angus told me, I dreamed about Nick's dad again.

Nick's friends from high school and college were gathered around the Wisemans' living room. We were talking about the time that Nick's dad, Pete, had invited us over in order to give us porcelain figures of a little white dog. These statuettes were meant to symbolize Willie, Nick's favorite dog.

Incidentally, Willie was the dog that curled up to Nick's body after he put a bullet in his brain. Willie was, presumably, trying to warm Nick up.

In the dream, my friend Josh said that it was a shame that Mr. Wiseman had died. I was confused because I had thought that Pete was still alive. So Josh showed me a letter he had kept that had accompanied the statue that Pete had given him.

I looked at the note and saw that it was some sort of postmodern poem. In it, Mr. Wiseman wrote this his wife was strong and that he was weak. He wrote that he had died in 2004. And he signed the note, "Guiltily, Pete."

All around me, Nick's friends were also reading copies of the note. It was a solemn moment. Josh looked at me and said, "It is a shame to lose somebody so young, isn't it?"

Though Mr. Wiseman was in his fifties when Nick took his life, Josh said, "He was only forty-five."

And then I woke up.

I kept writing.

***

I was the second person to arrive at Nick's parent's house, the morning that he put an AR-15 assault rifle into his mouth and pulled the trigger. Josh was the first.

I had been in class at the University of Minnesota working on my Master's in Education. My girlfriend at the time was in class with me. Her name was Julie. She was smart as a whip, cute as a cucumber, and crazier than a psych ward full of my mother's. She got a call from my friend Josh on her cell phone. Then, as now, I have avoided getting a cell phone.

Who wants to be that connected?

So I went out into the hallway to take the call. Josh told me that I needed to get over to Nick's house. He had killed himself last night. His voice was so shaky. I didn't trust myself to drive so Julie, my girlfriend at the time, drove me over to Nick's house.

Mr. Wiseman was outside smoking a cigarette when Julie and I got there. Josh was standing next to him. They weren't crying. They weren't talking. And so I stood with them.

Julie dropped me off and left. Later, after about six or seven guys who were close friends with Nick showed up, we sat in Nick's living room in complete silence. This lasted for five or six hours.

In our thirties, when Josh and I were talking after watching the German Videos, Josh remembered that Mrs. Wiseman had been vacuuming when he had arrived. Mr. Wiseman had been out front smoking a cigarette.

Incidentally, Mr. Wiseman had one of the deepest smoker's coughs I ever heard. He was in his sixties by the time I started writing this book. He spent much of his retirement on the porch of that same townhome where Nick killed himself, blowing perfect smoke rings into the sky.

Had Nick made it to his sixties, his smoker's cough would probably have been as deep. He really used to hack up a lung, even in his twenties.

Like adoptive father, like adopted son, right?

Anyway, when we arrived that morning, Mr. Wiseman told both Josh and I not to go into Nick's bedroom. That was where Nick had done it. That is where Mr. Wiseman found him with their two little, white dogs curled up against his cold body.

"Yoda and Willie knew something was wrong," Pete had said that morning.

"Why hadn't you?" Nick's mom asked me on the day of the funeral.

Nick's family had Yoda as long as I had known them. I remember when they bought Willie. He was tiny, white, and cute.

And both dogs had made cameos in the German videos we made together during high school. In one clip they were search dogs. In another they were wild animals. Willie even once played Pamela Anderson's dog.

When I reached for Pamela's ample chest, played by Josh with a stuffed shirt, Willie leapt at me in order to defend the sanctity of his owner against the lecherous TV host I was portraying that was based loosely off of the original Conan O'Brien show. We even had a cutaway shot to Max Weinberg smiling his way though a drum solo. We did all of this without the benefit of CGI or the Internet.

Anyway, when I had arrived at Nick's parent's house, I remember thinking that Mr. Wiseman was taking the situation well. He was gruff, to the point, and staying strong. Mrs. Wiseman, on the other hand, looked as though she were going to go downstairs, pick up the assault rifle, and follow Nick.

116

She looked very much like my mom had looked when I found her the morning that Jim shot himself.

As Nick's friends arrived on the day that he shot himself, we sat in silence in the Wiseman's living room. Nobody said a thing.

"I remember that it was so uncomfortable," my good friend Mike told me over breakfast, "I wanted to leave."

Or how about this?

"Didn't you just want to go downstairs and hang out with Nick?" This is what Josh said after we had dinner with Nick's parents.

Of course that was the feeling I got that night, at dinner with Nick's parents,

It was the similar feeling I got when I woke up after having a dream with Nick in it.

***

Did I say Julie was crazy? Here is a funny story about that particular ex-girlfriend of mine.

On the morning of Nick's funeral, as we were getting ready to leave, she locked herself in the bathroom of the garden level apartment that we shared. She took a butcher knife with her and threatened to kill herself. She did this because I asked her to wear a dress to Nick's funeral, she refused, and I got upset.

The irony of her threat emboldened me. I was ranting and raving. I yelled at Julie so loudly that an elderly woman knocked on our window to see if we were okay.

Finally, after talking Julie out of the bathroom and into her dress, we encountered the old woman on the steps. She was concerned and upset. She told Julie and I that she worked with abusive partners in relationships. She was pointing to me.

I responded by telling her that my best friend had killed himself, Julie had just threatened suicide, and I was trying to make my way to a funeral.

She was speechless. Whatever she was expecting me to say, this was not it. There was an awkward moment. I walked past her without a second glance.

Julie and I stopped traveling together soon after that.

She was nuts.

Hysterical stuff, am I right?

***

Last night, I was jolted out of another dream.

I had been in Nick's Cutlass Supreme. He had been driving. Josh was in the passenger seat. I was in the back.

And the car felt like a plane preparing for takeoff. Deathly afraid of flying, I started to panic. As I did so, I recognized Pearl Jam on the radio.

"I wish I were a sacrifice but somehow still lived on."

It was a line from the song, *Wishlist*. This was one of Nick's favorite songs. In fact, it was the album we listened to when he came to pick me up and move me home from the dorm rooms in his Cutlass Supreme.

And, before his car could take flight, I awoke from the dream.

And somehow, at thirty-two years old, I still lived on.

***

That next morning, I wrote about the song *Wishlist*.

Another line of that song went like this.

"I wish I were a neutron bomb, for once I could go off."

This line always reminded me of Nick, even before his suicide.

"Just bottle up all that rage Sam and then one day, boom! Explode, baby!"

All of us used to laugh when Nick made this joke. Nick laughed too. Whenever he was frustrated, he would say something to this effect.

Ten years ago, much like a neutron bomb, Nick went off. He did so by way of taking a shot at his head with an AR-15 assault rifle.

But maybe afterwards, he still lives on.

Afterall, once something is conjured, it doesn't go away.

There is a lesson in all of this. But as is the way with most good teaching and learning, a good lesson is a complicated process that takes time and must be experienced to be fully learned.

***

And I kept writing. And I kept dreaming.

In one dream, we were fourteen and my friends were divvying up football teams. Nick and I were split up. We often were.

We used to play football in the long driveway in front of Nick's parent's townhouse for hours. Nick and I would use our speed to go deep down the field. Due to this, we usually played opposite of each other. It was an appropriate matchup.

Mike or Josh or any of the other guys would sit back and throw deep balls over our shoulder. And when one of us scorched the other, we would playfully sneer at each other.

"That was luck."

"It was all skill, baby."

"I'm getting a hand on that next time."

"You gotta be faster you short, fat, Russian Jew."

"Watch me on the next down, slanty."

And we smiled and laughed with each other and lined up for the next play.

Yes and once something is conjured, it doesn't go away. I was friends with Nick, so so are you. Nick and I ran wild.

These sentences kept coming to me as I recounted my

dreams and my memories, as I imagined Nick, Magic, and I in the afterlife.

After lightning struck the first time, after Nick pulled the trigger, I continued living my life. I continued to travel. I became a high school English and Drama teacher. I got married. I drifted from twenty-two to thirty-two. Though I wish Nick had been around for all of that, oftentimes it felt as though Nick was still there with me, traveling.

Seeing Nick's parents, especially when they talked about the trips they had taken since Pete's retirement, I wondered if they hadn't given up traveling. There they were in that same house. Ten years later, whenever they see somebody that looks like Nick, they become petrified. Mr. Wiseman puts his hands in front of his mouth and looks away.

Mrs. Wiseman goes up and asks if she can touch their face.

***

But I was also writing for myself. In unearthing Nick in those mornings before school started, I found myself diving back into my own history. I started writing about myself. That is how I wrote what follows.

My grandmother died when I was seven. It was near the same time that my family's first dog, Muffy, died.

She didn't put a bullet in her brains. Natural causes did her in.

After we returned from the vet, I remember my sister's clueless grieving.

"Remember how Muffy used to sleep underneath the buffet? Isn't it sad?" Christie told my dad. He broke into tears and Mom told Christie to be quiet.

That same buffet is now in my living room. It was a gift to me from my father when I bought my house in Northeast Minneapolis. It was a gift to him from his mother when he and my mother bought a house in St.

Paul. My grandmother didn't have much, but she did have that buffet. So I have it now too.

I called my grandmother Bubbe. This was the Yiddish diminutive for grandma. She made delicious poppy seed cookies and smoked too much.

"She was a beautiful woman when she was younger," My father told me.

By the time I met her, she was a decrepit, wrinkled old woman.

The first time I went through college as a naïve English major, I wrote an epic poem about Bubbe escaping Russia as a little girl and coming to the lower east side of St. Paul as a Jewish immigrant. I was in my early twenties and had just read *Kaddish* by Allen Gingsberg. So I fancied myself an artist.

I walked upstairs to my father's office to show him the poem. At the time, I lived in the basement in a newer, more affluent suburban home. I was proud of my work and wanted to share it with him. Two days later, he brought the poem down to me in the basement. He had scribbled out many of my words and replaced them with his own.

"It works now," Dad told me.

I blew up at him. It was one of the few moments where, instead of hiding my anger away, I unloaded.

"That was *MY* poem," I told him, "it was wrong of you to change it."

He was hurt that I got so angry. I was so young.

Anyway, when I was seven, not long after Muffy and Bubbe died, my father and mother got divorced.

They pulled me out of first grade when it happened. The school counselor took me into their office.

"Are you upset?"

"No."

"You know your parents are getting divorced?"

"Yes."

"It is okay to be upset."

"I am fine."

"It is going to be fine."

"I know."

I responded to my counselor in the same way that Nick responded to his. I clammed up.

I *was* fine, though. I remember thinking that it was a good thing that my parents were getting divorced. Mom drank too much wine, Dad smoked too much pot, and all they did was scream at each other. All my sister did was misunderstand everything that was happening. All I did was turn on the television, plug in the Nintendo, and escape. Or I read. Or I went to a friend's house to escape. So it was better that Mom and Dad split up.

Anyway, I was writing about Bubbe.

Bubbe was chased out of the Ukraine as a little girl during the Russian Revolution. The Cossacks did not care for Jews. Her father, David, was a merchant. So he had enough money to book passage to America. David's wife died during the journey. So he raised my grandmother and her sister on the lower east side of St. Paul in relative poverty. Although, it must have been a step up from the dirt floors of the village where she grew up.

"When she made chicken noodle soup, she left the bone in the pot!" My mother later told me with disgust.

After my Bubbe's husband died, she grew depressed. My grandfather was fat, had a red face, and was a junk dealer. He was a Jewish immigrant from Russia as well. He never spoke to my father.

"The only time I saw any emotion, he was watching a televangelist on TV. He started to cry," my dad would say.

Even into his sixties, whenever my dad talked about his father, he would start to weep.

"Thank God that God is my real dad," he would say.

Anyway, after her husband died, my Bubbe was so depressed she started getting electro-shock therapy.

She was a first generation Jewish immigrant from Russia without hardly any money to her name in America.

122

I wonder why she was upset?

So they tried to shock some sense into her but it only made her worse.

Then my father, because his best friend had returned from Vietnam as a Jesus freak, agreed to pray in the name of Jesus to shut his friend up.

She stopped the therapy. She cheered up. My father became a Jesus freak. So I had to celebrate Christmas and Hanukah, Easter and Passover, white Lutheran values and Jewish immigrant values.

Talk about confusing!

And it only got more confusing from there.

But somewhere along the way I met Nick. And Nick was born in Korea and adopted by a staunch conservative father and an idealistic liberal mother and raised in the upper Midwest.

Nick and I had few cultural allegiances. That may have been one of the reasons we shared so many jokes at the sorts of people who took themselves and their identities so seriously. Nick and I couldn't afford that luxury.

I was told that Nick didn't write a suicide note. I was told that he scrawled "no funeral" on one side of a scrap of paper and "the art of crossing cultures" on the other.

For all I know, he wrote a novel and Nick's parents didn't share it with anybody. Nick was a prolific writer. His parents clutched everything that Nick was responsible for so tightly after he did himself in.

There was a funeral. As I wrote at the outset, I spoke at it. Years later, I found a copy of *The Art of Crossing Cultures*. According to our mutual friend Tricia, Nick had been reading that book prior to his suicide.

"Didn't you always feel bad for Nick? He clearly was in love with Tricia but he was too shy to tell her." My friend Mike told me over breakfast.

"He never got to have sex with a girl," Mike said, "isn't that sad?"

Reading *The Art of Crossing Cultures* left me frustrated. It was a broad psychological analysis of how people respond in new cultures. The book offered a series of steps that started with frustration, led to anger, and culminated in detachment.

Months after Nick read the book, his head became detached from his body.

As a thirty-two year old, I would like to be able to talk to Nick about that book. I felt it missed so many of the complexities of identity formation. As a doctoral student sifting through things like complexity and using phrases like identity formation, it would have been nice to bounce ideas off of Nick. He was so damned intelligent.

Figuring out how to be an American took its toll on Bubbe and Nick. It did so to my father and mother as well. It has been no easy ride for me either.

Ralph Ellison wrote that the American character is still in the womb. It hasn't been born yet. I liked that idea when I stumbled onto it as a doctoral student. All of *our* cultural heritages and identity formations could swirl about in a maelstrom of complexity and create a new identity. Perhaps, after a lobotomy by jackhammer, maybe a new sort of human could emerge, one that is more apt to travel peacefully with other humans. The *us* instead of the *me*, right? That could be some strong democracy.

That might be what I meant when I wrote the word *us* in italics throughout this book. It might also have something to do with the *them* that Magic had met and was trying to share with *us*.

Writing this book was so damned complicated.

***

I told my father I wanted to be a writer when I was eleven or twelve.

Books provided respite from being picked on at school, from listening to Dad yell at my sister Christie, from worrying about our absent mom and her pickling liver.

So I sat down and wrote a story that was two parts *The Stand* by Stephen King, one part *The Chronicles of Narnia* by C.S. Lewis, and ½ part my crazy dysfunctional childhood. It was about a tribe of humans surviving after a great apocalypse. Considering the apocalyptic nature of my childhood, this was fitting.

I showed Dad what I had written.

"This is good," he said.

What else could he say? What else did I want him to say? I wasn't sure, but I wanted somebody to tell me what happened next. Should I keep writing? Should I contact a publisher?

What should I do?

This was the question that stuck with me until I was thirty-two.

Writing this book about Nick seemed important. So I found a professional manuscript editor. I paid her $300 to read my manuscript about Nick. Later, I showed up at her house hoping she would answer the same question I posed to my father. A wonderfully warm woman, Mary invited me to sit at her dining room table. She poured me a cup of tea and told me this.

"Sam, this is two parts *Slaughterhouse Five* by Kurt Vonnegut, one part *I am America and So Can You* by Stephen Colbert, and ½ part *your* story about Nick. Give the reader you and Nick, Sam, that is all they need."

"What do I do next?" I asked her.

"You keep writing."

Mary gave me a hug as I left her house.

That was more than my father usually gave me.

***

Nick wrote a novella about me. He did this as a senior in Mr. Nelson's Creative Writing class. He rearranged my name so that it was Mas Rennat instead of Sam Tanner.

Incidentally, Mr. Nelson was a gnome of a man. Using

our accidentally acquired German, Nick and I referred to him as "Gartenzwerg." This meant garden gnome.

In his Creative Writing class, he shared a story he wrote. It was about his tour of duty in Vietnam. After relating the time that he killed a man with a knife to a group of horrified high school students, he did what he always did. He took the newspaper to his desk, put his feet up, and ignored us for the rest of the class period.

"Write something, will ya?" That was usually Mr. Nelson's lesson plan.

My friend Mike took Mr. Nelson's class as a senior.

"There is a picture of him with a Gatling gun on his bulletin board," Mike had laughed.

"Creepy, right?" I had said.

When it came time for Mike to turn in a portfolio of poetry for Mr. Nelson, I printed out what I had written the previous year when I took his course. My work included a name poem about Tony the Tiger, the advertising face of Frosted Flakes. The only comment Mr. Nelson gave me about my writing was written next to that poem.

"G-g-g-g-g-reat!" He wrote.

When Mike turned in my poetry with his name written on it the next year, he got the same grade that I did.

Clearly Mr. Nelson did not put much thought into reading our work. I did not emulate Mr. Nelson in my own teaching. Later, when I taught my first section of Creative Writing, I vowed to read every word my students wrote. Talk about exhausting, but I did it.

Creative Writing was one of the few classes that I got an A in during my time in high school. This was mostly due to Mr. Nelson's disinterest, my aspirations as an author, and my general disinterest in Math, Science, whatever.

Nick got an A in Mr. Nelson's class as well.

I always remembered the final line of Mr. Nelson's story about Vietnam.

"And that was the last day that I was ever young."

Mr. Nelson classified his story under the genre of therapeutic writing. As much as I'd liked to think that I avoided learning anything from that man, here I am playing with that genre myself.

Anyway, in the story that Nick wrote for Mr. Nelson, I had a son named Sam. He started his own religion. Nick was toying with the Dune story as Mas built an army of Amazonian soldiers and took over the fictional universe that Nick dreamed up.

Katie and I had been trying to have a child since our wedding. This was to no avail. So Nick's depiction of my son stood painfully out to me as I read his work.

After a year and a half of trying to make a son with my wife Katie, it saddened me to see this vision of my future in Nick's work.

Anyway, Nick's career as a writer ended when he put a bullet in his brain.

Here I am trying to pick up where he left off.

- CHAPTER 10 -

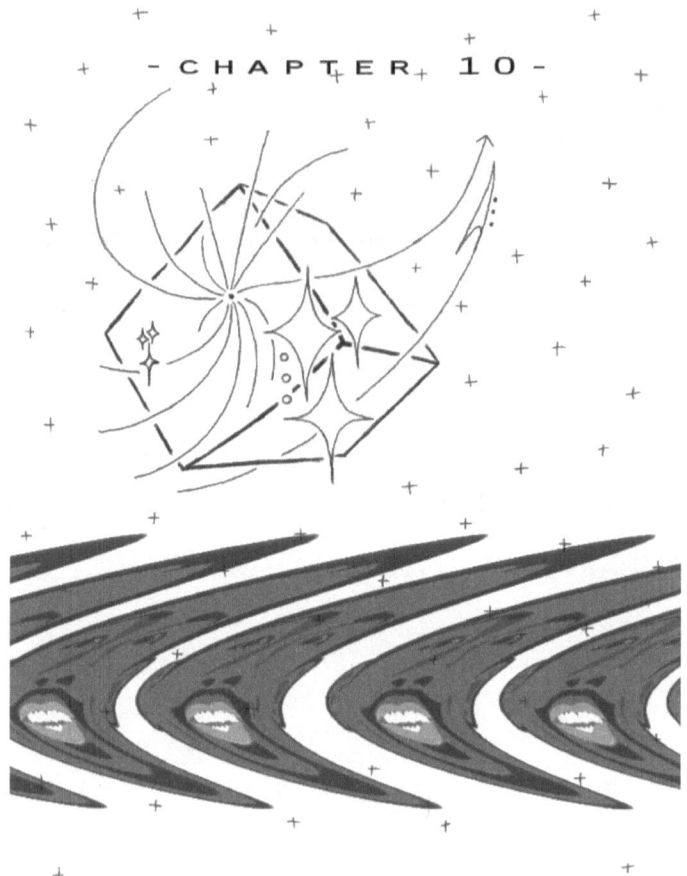

The only thing that I have ever shot and killed was a prairie dog. Though I tried to miss, I took its head off with an AR-15 assault rifle.

Incidentally, Nick used that same gun to take his own head off.

When I was thirteen, Nick and his parents took me with them on a road trip to Montana. Thirsty for familial stability, the trip was a reprieve. My father was busy getting stoned and losing his temper. My absent mother was drinking herself silly with my then-living stepfather Jim. My sister was a hurricane. The trip offered me an escape.

Nick's parents paid my way. And I loved the big, open spaces of Montana. It was a blast trading cassette tapes with Nick. He had a copy of Alice n' Chains *Jar of Flies* and I let him listen to Pearl Jam's *Ten*. In the car, we listened to our Walkmans in the backseat, laughed like fools, and watched the scenery pass. When we stopped to eat or to sleep, Nick's parents footed the bill.

Imagine the expense of adopting an orphan from Korea and raising that child as their own. Nick's parents were very much like Nick. They gave whatever they had to give. To hear them speak of it, both of them came from poor families. And in the same way that Nick would spend his last dollar to make sure you ate if you were out with him at Perkins in high school, Nick's parents made sure that I had enough to eat on the road trip to Montana and, for that matter, every time I rode the bus home with Nick during middle school.

One morning, we woke up early to go prairie dog hunting. Mr. Wiseman was a soldier, a policeman, and an avid hunter. He was a Robert Heinlein novel.

"Guns don't kill people," he would say, "people do."

Or how about this?

"The only polite society is an armed society."

Mostly Nick would agree with his father, unless, of course, they were face to face. Then Nick would make it a point to bicker about whatever he could think of to bicker about.

"Did you remember to pack lunch, Nick?"

"Of course I did, father. Did you remember the ammo? You forgot to bring extra ammo the last time we went hunting."

"My ass I did."

"Your ass is right."

"Just check to make sure you packed lunch."

"You check, jackass."

"Don't be an asshole."

In my memory, the two blur. Nick may have been a Korean orphan, but he had more in common with that white, conservative, mid-western cop than anybody else. Both men were stubborn, held rigid ideological beliefs, and were deeply perceptive.

Driving out to Montana as a thirteen year old, I respected both of them a great deal. I suppose I respected them long after Nick put a bullet in his brain, as Pete retired and nursed his smoker's cough, as Nick came to me in my dreams. Both of them were fierce human beings.

But almost twenty years ago we drove to Montana together, woke up early one morning, and went prairie dog hunting.

After an hour of driving, we were in the middle of nowhere. Mr. Wiseman had met a farmer in the hotel bar the night before who had agreed to let us go out to his ranch and shoot prairie dogs.

I still shudder at the ruthlessness of this act. We set up Mr. Wiseman's AR-15 assault rifle a fair distance from the prairie dog hill. The critters were popping out of holes, chattering playfully, and going about their morning. It was a beautiful, sunny day in an open field. Mr. Wiseman attached the scope to his weapon.

After Nick and his dad took turns strafing the hill, they told me to give it a try. As a thirteen-year old boy, androgynous enough with my long hair and baby's face, I felt obliged to participate in what I then perceived to be the masculine ritual of gunning down prairie dogs.

Did I say androgynous? When we stopped at a restaurant to use the restroom on that same trip, the waitress pointed Nick one way and me the other. Nick thought that my mistaken gender was hysterical. Later, both he and I used the Bob Seger song *Turn the Page* to fondly remember when that waitress was unsure of my gender. Was I a woman or a man?

Nick and I saw Bob Seger in concert at the Target Center in Minneapolis when we were thirteen. It was the first concert I ever went to. Nick's parents bought us tickets.

"Look at all of these old people," he had said at the time.

"Are you watching them dance?"

They were gyrating their flabby hips. It was deeply unpleasant to watch. Later, we saw Pearl Jam at the same venue with our friend Josh. We sat behind the stage. Eddie Veddar raged and rambled all over that stage, crooning "Release Me!" into the terrible acoustics of that space. It was one of the final things that Nick and I did together before he pulled the trigger.

I digress.

I had never fired a gun before and so I was nervous as I took position. I looked into the scope. There was a prairie dog, dancing and playing in the morning sun. Its naïve innocence was heartbreaking.

Nick and his dad bickered as I broke into a sweat.

"Just take aim and squeeze the trigger."

"Let him do it, Dad."

"Don't be a jackass, Nick."

"Moron."

I knew what I had to do. I aimed the gun slightly away from the prairie dog. I couldn't kill this defenseless creature. And I squeezed the trigger. And I watched in horror as the recoil bucked the rifle and the prairie dog exploded in the scope.

"Shit!"

"Did he hit it?"

Nick and his dad raced over to the hill. I joined them. There was the bloody corpse of a prairie dog. I had taken its head off.

"What a shot!"

"Wow."

I felt terrible the rest of the day.

To add insult to this unnecessary injury, while I was setting up behind the gun, I sat directly on a cactus.

"He sat ass-backwards on a cactus," Mr. Wiseman later told Mrs. Wiseman with a laugh. "He pulled down his shorts right there on the highway and I had to pick cactus out of his butt with a tweezers."

Needless to say, my male initiation into the art of firing assault rifles only further complicated my androgyny.

It was nice of Mr. Wiseman to clean out my backside, right? He often related the story in my presence. And he always laughed like a fool as he recounted the incident. Here I will mention that Mr. Wiseman once paid me five dollars to eat a habanera pepper. I nearly puked. He laughed his ass off. Wasn't that nice of him? Well, it *was* funny.

I digress.

And that prairie dog was the only thing that I have ever shot with an assault rifle. I'll be damned if I didn't use the same AR-15 that Nick turned on himself when he was twenty-two. Nick, much like that prairie dog, lost his head.

Talk about unnecessary injury.

***

In seventh grade Nick loaned me his father's copy of *The Puppet Masters* by Robert Heinlein. I read it in one sitting. I even called Nick later that night to talk to him about it.

Nick was one of the few intelligent readers I knew as

an adolescent.

Last night, as a thirty-two year old, I picked *The Puppet Masters* off the shelf and read it. Again, I did it in one sitting.

As a thirty-two year old, I noticed how fiercely Heinlein advocated for his version of independent living and thinking. His protagonists were at odds with peaceful, social collaboration. So much so that in *The Puppet Masters*, the honorable humans are trying to blow up an organism that is essentially an ultimate form of social organization. Dare I mention communism?

The book was still candy to me as an adult. I've read enough science fiction from that era to fill a landfill. This is thanks to Nick and Nick's father's bookshelf in their basement.

About six months prior to my second reading of *The Puppet Masters*, I had finished the one-act about Nick. In it, we were playing poker in a dream. It was ten years after he had committed suicide and we were trying to make sense of each other. Incidentally, I mentioned Heinlein in the play as well. My friend that staged the play a couple of months later had this to say.

"Sam," he said, "I am starting to grok the script a little bit better now."

My friend had read Robert Heinlein as well.

And he also had this to say.

"I think the play is less about exploring Nick's suicide, and more of a memorial for him. That seems to fit where you are in the grieving process."

"Yeah?"

"You are still early in the process."

"I have had ten years to deal with it."

"Yeah, but that was an enormous thing to deal with."

"Yeah?"

"What do I know? But that is what I saw as I staged it."

My friend wanted me to dig deeper in the script. It was short and only touched delicately on the contextual factors surrounding Nick, his suicide, and me.

Anyway, reading *The Puppet Masters* a second time was another exploration of Nick, his suicide, and me. It was also as an act of memorial for him.

In many ways, it was the opposite of unnecessary injury. It was, for me, an act of necessary travel.

Instead of putting a bullet in anything, I wrote a play. And then I started to write this.

***

Incidentally, whenever Nick was angry with stupid people, and he was often angry with stupid people, he would say that somebody needed to teach them a lesson.

This happened most often when Nick was driving. Somebody would cut him off or somebody would be driving too slowly in front him. And Nick would race up behind the culprit or whip around the driver that had cut him off and return the favor. When asked why he was being so reckless, he would reply that somebody needed to teach the moron a lesson.

When Nick would cross the street and a car were driving too slowly, too quickly, or without paying attention, Nick would walk right into it. Invariably this horrified the driver and those of us who were with Nick.

"What are you doing?"

"Gotta teach that moron a lesson."

A moron, for Nick, was anybody who got in the way of how he imagined people should live or be. In this way, Nick was very much like a Robert Heinlein book.

When I told him that he was acting like a jackass?

"You are a moron, Sam."

That was that.

***

In eighth grade Nick and I read the Dune series in its

entirety.

His father had the books on his shelf. There was a veritable arsenal of science fiction to work through. Nick was a vigorous reader. He learned to navigate that armory of books as well as he learned to work the stockpile of his dad's guns in the closet underneath the stairs.

With nothing else to do in middle school, I read with him. He loaned me the books.

"Don't ruin this one, jackass."

I used to read in the bath. Oftentimes I would return Nick's books and they would have watermarks on the pages. He would notice.

"Who reads in the bath, moron?"

I did. Closing the door to the bathroom, filling the tub with hot water, and diving into a book created a wonderful escape from the chaos of my dad and my sister on the other side of the door.

One of my favorite reads from the Dune series was *The God Emperor of Dune*. In fact, I picked it up recently to scan through it.

The fourth in the *Dune* series, the book related the story of a four thousand year old Worm Emperor named Leto that contains all of the memories of the human race. After committing atrocities in the name of keeping political order and shaping the long-term survival of the human race, the Worm Emperor tells its advisor that part of its purpose was teach the human race a lesson through its actions.

When I reread that line as a thirty-two year old, I thought about Nick.

In remembering Nick, my good friend Mike recalled how both he and Nick would joke that their purpose in life was to teach the human race a lesson. I can only assume that Nick acquired this missive in our adolescent reading and that he later shared it with Mike.

For them, this meant retaliating whenever they were a victim of what they deemed injustice or stupidity. I remember him being cut off on the freeway or standing behind people in lines.

Mike and Nick were angry in their pedagogy. Nick was quick to call somebody a jackass or a moron and Mike, when he disagreed with a call on the basketball court, was infamous for getting technical fouls. In fact, as sophomores in our intramural league at the University of Minnesota, Mike led the league in technical fouls. I once saw him kick a basketball halfway across the gym after disagreeing with a call. The ref tossed him from the game. I think that was one of the only ejections in the history of intramural ball at the University.

After sharing this memory of Nick's mantra, Mike told me over breakfast that he had been working to change that philosophy. In fact, he has taken to reffing high school basketball games. At thirty-two, Mike seemed to be learning the futility in enacting such angry pedagogy as a way of living.

Nick didn't learn this lesson. At twenty-two, he put a bullet in his brains. He did this in his bedroom, a hallway removed from his father's arsenal of arms and literature.

In talking about Nick and Nick's dad, I was quick to borrow Mr. Wiseman's line that he borrowed from a Robert Heinlein book.

"Guns don't kill people," I say, "people kill people."

Of course, people make guns, people write books, and Nick had access to both. And Nick was people and so were his parents.

When Mrs. Wiseman used to hear Mr. Wiseman argue the side of the NRA, she would roll her eyes and talk about the importance of gun control. She was a feisty liberal.

The Wiseman marriage was microcosm of the split in American politics today. Mr. Wiseman was a staunch conservative and Mrs. Wiseman was a stubborn liberal. Nick, like all of us Americans today, was the offspring of this polarization in political ideology.

Did all of that opposition kill Nick?

"How the hell would you know?" Nick said in the final line of the one-act play that I wrote about him. After he said this, he took the AR-15 assault rifle from the character that represented me in the play and walked off stage.

I know when Nick and I read *The God Emperor of Dune* in middle school that he understood it better than me. He grokked it, as it were. Nick was fiercely intelligent. Whether it was disassembling Tecmo Super Bowl, reading science fiction, or playing poker, Nick's intelligence was something to behold.

At thirty-two, in rereading *The God Emperor of Dune,* I couldn't stop thinking about what Nick had been thinking about when Leto, this ultimate intellect, turned to his advisor and said the following.

"My purpose is to teach the human race a lesson that they will never forget."

One of Nick's fiercest beliefs was the stupidity of censorship. His mother was always worried about Nick playing violent video games, listening to Ozzy Osbourne or watching *Fight Club*. Nick would angrily assert the importance of free speech. In fact, one of the few assignments he completed in high school was a thoughtful research paper arguing against censorship. If I agreed with Nick vehemently that it was wrong to censor ideas back then, I agreed with him even more as I got older.

If I had the chance, I wouldn't go back and censor Dune out of his or my reading list. I don't think that violent or dark texts made Nick commit suicide. Frankly, I would sooner blame the repression of Nick's thoughts and feelings than anything else.

But what do I know? I am still traveling. I am still trying to get smart.

***

I stumbled into John Dewey during my doctoral work.

He believed that people learned through doing. For Dewey, meaningful learning came through experiences. Though Dewey's prolific academic career is still relevant in academic circles, American public schools still put their faith in multiple-choice tests instead of Dewey's idea of democratic education.

In *The God Emperor of Dune,* Leto claimed he was a tyrant in order to teach the human race the necessity for independent and democratic or liberatory thinking. His author, Frank Herbert, allowed him to put on the skin of a sandworm and to live for four thousand years. It would take at least that long, Herbert assumed, to teach such a lesson. Leto's tyranny allowed for the continuation of the human race. And it made for a great piece of 20th century science fiction.

In my memory, Nick's parents were both caring and disciplined. Oftentimes, they would impose their discipline on Nick. They pushed Nick to do the things that they thought he ought to do. This meant that, until 8th grade, Nick got straight A's. In about 8th grade, Nick started to rebel from what he perceived to be his parent's tyranny. His grades started to slip. About ten years later, he used his father's AR-15 assault rifle to put a bullet in his head on his mother's birthday.

I often wondered if Nick's performance was his attempt to do to his parents what he did to slow drivers on the freeway, teach them a lesson. And, borrowing from John Dewey and Leto, I wonder if Nick understood he was trying to deploy the notion of experiential education?

***

I have a motivational speech that I give on the first day of any high school class that I have taught. I told a story to set the stage for what was in front of us. It involved building a house of cards.

I told a story about watching a girl build a house of

cards in a study hall. I described how the classroom full of people were relentless in trying to knock it down.

The gist of the lesson was that we had a semester of experiences in front of us and, regardless of how many things interfered with our cardhouse, I wanted my students to continue building with me. Furthermore, I didn't want them to destroy each other's work or, for that matter, each other. I wanted them to be kind.

A student once told me that the power of my story had nothing to do with my delivery.

"If somebody just sees you screaming and waving your hands around about cardhouses, they don't get it. They need to be there, working with you for three months to get it. You never give up. You just keep building cardhouses with whoever is in the room with you, regardless of what is happening."

That, to me, was experiential learning.

The experience I tried to simulate was that of a group of people trying to build something together instead of destroying things.

***

I guess Nick and I were different sorts of teachers.

***

Nick's mom was a different sort of teacher too.

The summer after seventh grade, I spent a great deal of time at Nick's house playing Nintendo, drinking Mountain Dew, and staying cool. Nick's mom began to worry that he and I were atrophying. When Nick's mom started worrying about something, she very earnestly set to task.

After a great deal of bickering between Nick and his mother, we agreed to jog to the gas station about a mile away in exchange for five dollars each. Nick's mom was delighted.

It was humid and hot, and Nick and I set out from his front door. Each of us had been athletic at one time or another and so we hit the run with gusto. In fact, the skill that made Nick and I valuable on the football field or on the basketball court was our speed and so running seemed to follow suit.

About two minutes into the run, Nick was wheezing. I was tired too but I was planning on completing the task that was given to me. Nick, on the other hand, was quick to opt out. So when Nick stopped running and started walking, I did the same. He was exhausted.

"Let's just walk."

"Are you sure?"

"Yes."

So we walked to the gas station, bought two bottles of pop, and wheezed our way back to Nick's Nintendo.

"You guys make it?" Nick's mother asked.

"Yes, mother. Now leave us alone." Nick growled.

And Nick and I proceeded to play Nintendo.

Twenty years later, I was diligently chasing my doctorate and completing tasks as they were given to me. Nick was an atrophying lump of flesh in the earth.

***

I read a story on BBC.com last year. The story reminded me of Nick.

A middle-aged woman taught middle school in England. She was fed up with her students. Imagine that moment when the chaos, whatever chaos bothers you most, consumed you. For me, I remember my first year supervising a 9th grade study hall. I hid in a book as the students rolled dice in the back, tried to procreate with each other, and committed unspeakable acts of cosmic atrocity against each other. I often painted that study hall in metaphorical broad strokes as I told my story about building cardhouses. I said that those students lit the

140

classroom on fire. Speaking of fire, one day, during recess, the middle-aged teacher in the story doused herself in gasoline and lit a match. She burned up in front of her students.

Imagine their horror. As she was going up in flames, she told them to let her burn. Is there a more dramatic way to express frustration? I cannot think of one.

Well, maybe putting a bullet in one's head, yes?

When I was feeling silly or grotesque, I sometimes shared one of my teaching fantasies with a class. This was only if the class and I had built meaningful things and, therefore, had a cosmic connection. The fantasy was this.

It is the first period of the first day of 9th grade English. As an old man, I walk in front of the class in order to start the students on their path through public high school. And all of a sudden my heart starts shuddering, explodes, and blood starts spewing from my mouth, ears, and my eyes. And maybe my fingertips too. And my knees. And my toes. Something truly horrifying, you know?

Imagine how those kids would react! They would never forget it! Unlike so many of the worksheets, tests, and other monotonous tasks that they would accomplish in school, this would be a moment that would be forever etched in their brains.

This fantasy made me laugh. It usually made my students laugh too, after they get used to the playfulness and harmlessness of my dark sense of humor.

I have seen a great deal of dark stuff and so my sense of humor is dark. It is hard for me to separate who I am from my teaching, from my living, and, I guess, from my writing.

Nick's teaching happened with an assault rifle. I guess it was hard for him to separate himself as well. To his credit, his act is etched in my head forever. The same is true of my friends Mike, Josh, and Nick's parents. They will never forget Nick's lesson.

I wonder what those students in England were learning

as their teacher went up in flames during recess?

***

About a year before Nick killed himself, he called me at three in the morning. He needed a ride home from a party in Minneapolis.

"Come pick me up."

"Nick, it is three in the morning. I have to go to work in three hours."

I was a weekend manager at Subway. At the time, I was finishing up my undergraduate degree in English at the University of Minnesota and putting in 40 hours a week at my Job. Nick, on the other hand, had long since dropped out of college and was unemployed. He was drifting.

"Just come get me, I have nobody else to call."

I swore into the phone, hung up, and struggled out of bed.

As much as I was pissed off at Nick, I knew that he would have gotten out of bed to pick me up. In fact, during our freshmen year of college, I had been forced to give him a call.

I had been rooming with Mike and Josh. After three months in Pioneer Hall, I decided I couldn't do it anymore. I needed to move home. Mike and Josh had started to cut strips off of my green blanky, my baby blanket. I referred to it affectionately as Blanky Bob. They would hang the strips above our dorm room door so that I couldn't reach them. They thought it was funny. And I guess it was. But I had had enough. And I missed my girlfriend. I missed my privacy. I wanted to move back home to my parent's basement. So I called Nick and he was immediately on his way over to help me cart my stuff away in his 1980 Cutlass Supreme station wagon.

His Cutlass smelled of old man. Its previous owner had been a rugged carpenter. So Nick would spray orange air freshener to get rid of the scent. But instead of covering up the scent, the orange air freshener mingled with it. Nick's Cutlass smelled of orange B.O. It was horrifying.

But the car was big enough so that I could jam my television, my books, and the remains of my green blanky into the back.

When I called Nick, he was over in twenty minutes to help me pack. My good friends Mike and Josh sat in angry silence as I announced that I was leaving. Josh sat on the couch staring at the empty space on the TV stand after I loaded my television into Nick's car. Josh didn't say a word as I packed the last of my stuff. Mike and Josh didn't talk to me for three months afterwards. It took awhile, but our friendships survived.

Nick was always there when I needed something. So when he called me for a ride at three in the morning, I felt obligated.

When I got there, Nick was alone on the curb outside of a packed house. He didn't know anybody at the party. The people he had come with had long since left.

"What the hell, Nick?"

"Thanks for coming to get me. You want to come inside and have a drink?"

"No, I don't. I have to work in three hours. Just get in the car."

"Fine, be a Debbie Downer."

I silently fumed.

Nick got in the car. I was pissed. I was tired. So I started in.

"What is your problem, Nick?"

"What do you mean?"

"It is three in the morning. You are at some stupid ass party in Minneapolis without a ride home. You don't have a job. You aren't going to school. What are you doing with your life?"

"Great, you are going to get on your high horse, now? Almighty Sam and his God complex?"

This was a favorite phrase of Nick's. Whenever I

started getting high and mighty with advice, this was his defense mechanism.

"*You* are the one who called *me*, so here I am. Tell me, why are you throwing your life away?"

"…"

Nick got angry.

"Why are you so angry all the time?"

Nick grew quiet. And both of us grew angrier. For one of the few times in our post-adolescent relationships, I pressed him. I wanted to know why he was making the choices that he was making. I wanted to know why he wouldn't talk about his feelings. He became sullen. I became determined to make him talk. Finally, he opened his mouth.

"You want to know what is wrong, Sam?"

"Yes!"

"Fine, I'll tell you."

"Finally."

"But first you need to stop and buy me McDonalds."

"Christ, I need to bribe you?"

"You are the one that wants to know."

So I stopped and bought that manipulative prick McDonalds. After all, I was the one with money in my pockets. I had a job that I had to be at in a couple of hours. As I handed him the bag of food, I told him that he couldn't eat in my car. So he started munching on fries anyways.

Incidentally, we were riding in my 1994 Honda Civic. This was the first car that I bought myself. Unlike my previous car, a 1984 Cutlass Cierra that maxed out at 50 mph, it was well maintained.

Nick ate. Nick was silent. And then Nick started to talk to me.

"My dad did something that I couldn't forgive. "

"Okay."

Nick was speaking through a mouthful of French fries.

"I was on a hunting trip with my dad. We were in

Alaska. He told me something. I could not forgive him for it."

There was seriousness in the car now.

"What was it?"

"I can't tell you that."

"What did he do?"

"I can't tell you that."

"..."

"..."

A silence hung heavy as I turned into Nick's parent's driveway.

And we got to Nick's house. And Nick got out of the car. And I drove home and woke up for work that morning.

A year later Nick was dead.

***

Nick called me a week before he shot himself. It was odd because I hadn't heard from him for some time.

I was busy finishing my teacher's license at The University of Minnesota. I was busy with the crazy girl I was dating at the time, Julie. So when he asked me if I wanted to get together and play Madden, I thought it was a little strange.

"Sure, that would be great," I said. But I didn't really mean it. Because I was too busy with all of the other things I was too busy with.

A week later Nick took his head off with the same AR-15 assault rifle that I had used to kill that harmless prairie dog.

- CHAPTER 11 -

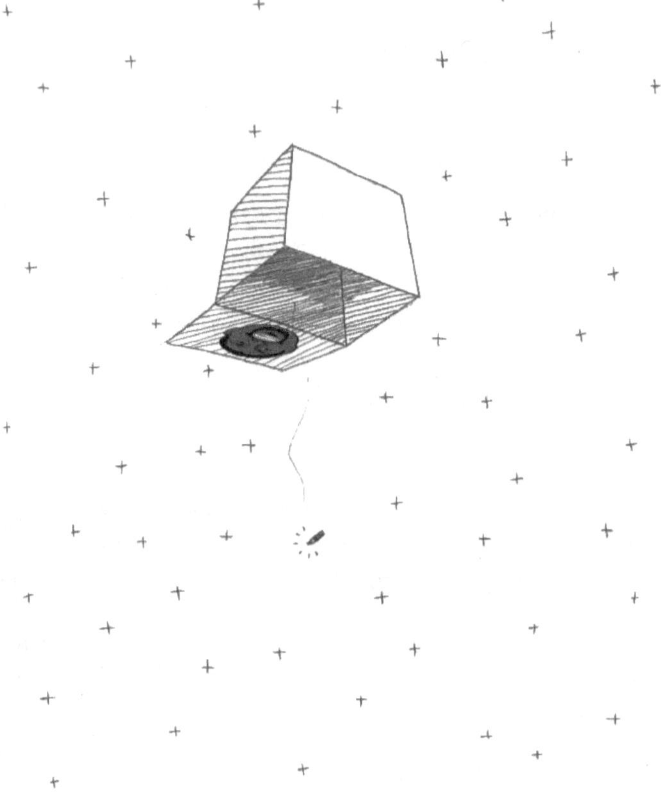

Above the River Styx, the sky turned crimson. The little wooden boat in the middle of the river shuddered. Electricity hung heavy in the air. Clouds began to rumble.

Inside of the boat, Nick, Sam, and Magic huddled together. An enormous, complicated universe spread out around them. Sam was nervous. Nick was ambivalent. Magic was glowing with anticipation.

And then *it* happened.

The sky opened up. The first bolt of lightning struck Nick and Sam simultaneously. The second bolt did the exact same thing.

Magic "Fucking" Johnson let out a laugh the filled that space between spaces.

"They've arrived, gentleman, *they've* come to take us *there,"* Magic's laughter was thunder.

A great flash of light occurred. They were caught up in that flash. And then they were surrounded by white light.

It was accomplished. *They* had reached *their* destination. Yes, *they* were *there*.

***

There in that glow, Sam and Nick appeared to each other in a boogie land of sorts.

For the first time in quite some time, *they* saw each other clearly. There was nothing between *them* anymore. Both Sam and Nick laughed loudly. *Their* laughter illuminated the space. *They* were surrounded by infinite universe. In fact, *they* were infinite universe. *They* almost resembled twelve beings of inordinate light. *They* also resembled what they used to be.

So Sam was wearing a black, Pearl Jam t-shirt. He had buckteeth and long hair. He was short and pudgy and thirteen years old. His face was red. It was, as Nick had often pointed out to him when they played football on those cold, October nights, splotchy.

Nick used to tell Sam that his white skin was like a

hypercolor shirt. When it was cold outside or when Sam was embarrassed, his skin would change color. Hypercolor shirts were popular when Sam and Nick first met in the early nineties, when they were children. The shirts changed color with a change in temperature, if you touched them. So this was a joke that Nick would make at Sam's expense. Sam would laugh like a fool about it.

Sam was often embarrassed when the other thirteen year olds made fun of his blotchy skin or pudgy face. When Nick did it, it seemed to make things better.

But Sam was also dressed in a sweater vest. And he had spiked his short hair with gel as was the fashion. He was also skinny as was the fashion. He was thirty-two years old as well as thirteen.

Nick was wearing a purple Minnesota Vikings shirt. His jeans were too tight and he was skinny and short. He was thirteen years old.

Unlike Sam, Nick's skin never changed colors. This was because he was born in Korea. Sam would squint his eyes and ask Nick if he wanted any rice. This was meant to be a retort to the joke that Nick would make at Sam's expense. And Nick would laugh like a fool. There was nothing mean about Sam's joke.

But Nick was also a shadowy, stern figure. His eyes seemed distant as though he had seen something that was impossible to communicate in this iteration of the English language. There was a hole in his head and dirt on his face. He was thirty-two years old as well thirteen.

"Nick," Sam said.

"Sam," Nick said.

A memory of Mrs. Wiseman came to Sam. She had so badly wanted to touch Nick one more time. Sam looked Nick in the eye. Nick's eyes were heavier. They understood something that Sam didn't about people deciding to put bullets in their brains. Nick and Sam took a moment to take each other in. *They* shared what *they* had since become with each other.

Sam shivered. He reached out to touch Nick. For the first time in the entirety of their relationship, *they* touched. Sam gently put his hand on Nick's shoulder. Electricity ran up and down *their* spines.

At that moment, they transformed entirely.

And *they* finally saw Magic "Fucking" Johnson for what he was. So they also saw Earvin Johnson for what he had been.

Earvin Johnson was also thirteen years old. He was wearing an old 1987-88 Los Angeles Lakers t-shirt. It was too small for him. He was chubby and afraid.

A group of boys were gathered around him. One of them shoved Earvin.

"Earvin Johnson?" They laughed. "Like the basketball player? What a fucking joke." Earvin hung his head in shame.

But in the same moment, Earvin Johnson was also Magic "Fucking" Johnson because *they* were *them* and *they* were *there*. So Magic was an electrical storm. He was a note conjured by a flute. He was two big, smiling eyes. He was the ability to travel peacefully regardless of circumstance. He was infinity. He was woosh.

Sam and Nick, as thirty two year olds, turned to Earvin as a thirteen year old.

"Who are you?" Thirty-two year old Sam asked.

"Earvin," thirteen-year old Earvin said.

"What are you doing here?"

"I don't know." Earvin was afraid.

Sam looked from Earvin to Nick and back again.

"It is going to be *okay*, Earvin."

"How do you know?" Earvin was afraid.

Something dawned on Sam.

"I just do. We are *here*. And *this* is a safe space. In fact, it is the only safe space. If we can figure out how to bring *here* everywhere with us, then we can have the courage to travel." Sam was confident.

Nick looked from Sam to Earvin and back again.

"Like Magic "Fucking" Johnson, baby." Nick said. For the first time since he put a bullet in his head, Nick was really Nick again. His cackle was reckless, sarcastic, and full of good-natured humor.

Nick's statement made Earvin smile. Sam responded in kind.

"Like Magic "Fucking" Johnson, baby." After Earvin said this, he seemed to fade into Magic "Fucking" Johnson. The beings blurred.

They were shifting through time and space together because both of those things are meaningless. There is nothing so specific, *there*.

Magic turned to Sam and Nick as thirteen-year olds.

"Who are you?" Thirteen-year old Sam asked.

"I am Magic "Fucking" Johnson," Magic said.

"The basketball player?" Nick asked.

"Maybe." Magic smiled.

Sam and Nick were afraid.

Magic looked from Sam to Nick and back again.

"It is going to be okay, guys."

"How do you know?"

"*You* told me so. In fact, *you* showed me so. *You* showed me like *this*."

And Magic smiled. His grin stretched into infinity. He was speaking with something that was stronger than his head, his heart. He was teaching *them*.

Magic blinked his eyes and found himself a million miles above the surface of the earth. He was in a hot air balloon. He blinked his eyes again and Nick and Sam were with him.

"What the hell is happening?" Nick called out.

"We are traveling, so so are you!"

Now Sam blinked his eyes and he, Nick, and Magic were standing at a gravesite.

"Where are we now?" Nick noticed a tombstone.

It read as follows. Nicholas L. Wiseman, June 23, 1979 - September 4, 2002.

Sam looked at Nick. Nick couldn't believe it. He started to laugh. So did Magic. Sam joined in. Sam blinked his eyes again. The tombstone changed to read as follows: Kilgore Trout, 1965-2007. It was the alter ego of another of Sam's psychopomps, Kurt Vonnegut. And Vonnegut had recently kicked the proverbial can as well.

"What a pity!"

Sam was laughing hysterically now. And his laughter blended with tears.

Now Nick blinked his eyes and the tombstone changed to read as follows. James T. Schultz, March 8th, 1946 – January 26th, 2011.

"Suicide is a motherfucker, right Nick?" Sam asked.

"It has fucked some mothers." Nick said.

"Yours?"

"Mine."

"Mine too."

"Ha!"

"You know the real bitch about suicide, Nick?"

"What?"

"Once something is conjured, it does not go away. Ever."

"What a barrel of monkeys."

Sam blinked his eyes. And then a million barrels surrounded them. Each barrel contained two monkeys.

The three of them laughed loudly. As they did so, a dinosaur ran wild through the barrels of monkeys. A young woman followed the dinosaur. She was wearing a wedding veil. Her wedding veil was white. She was not white. Neither was Nick. But that didn't matter at all in *the place*. Anyways, a high school administrator chased the young woman. She might have been white. Who cares?

Nick looked at Sam and started laughing so hard that he was crying. Sam did the same. Magic joined in.

"Are any of us white?" Magic asked this with a smile.

"Fuck that!" Nick's cigarette was burning wildly.

Sam blinked his eyes. And he, Nick, and Magic were in

Nick's basement. They were playing *Genghis Khan* on Nick's Nintendo. Nick's mom was upstairs. She was making the boys dinner.

"Dinner will be ready in fifteen minutes, boys."

"Thank you, mother."

Nick handed the controller to Sam. Sam organized his armies, trained his princes, and handed the controller to Magic. Magic asked Sam and Nick how to play.

"Just blink your eyes, baby."

The three of *them* blinked *their* eyes together again.

Sam was sitting on a half-moon crescent. Magic and Nick were sitting with him. They were a million miles above the earth. A billion. Whatever.

"Have either of you read the play, *No Exit* by Sartre?" Sam was thinking out loud.

Earvin and Nick shrugged.

"In it, three people are trapped together for eternity in the afterlife. The famous line is Hell is other people, right? Wrong. Hell is other people that cannot travel together like *us*. Watch this."

Sam blinked his eyes and he, Nick, Magic, and their good friends Mike and Josh were on a basketball court together. And suddenly it was a game of basketball. Unlike the way they played as children, this was a good game.

Sam was bringing the ball up the court. He was playing point. Nick was at his side. Nick was the shooting guard. Mike was playing small forward. Josh took power forward. And Magic "Fucking" Johnson was playing center. Of course, Magic could play whatever position he liked.

Now *they* were playing basketball with the universe.

"And this wasn't the sort of basketball that Nick and I played when we were thirteen," Sam later wrote, "this was the sort of basketball being played by people who knew what it was to win some, knew what it was to lose some, and knew what is was to travel through time and space as the flow of the game allowed."

But Sam wrote that later. He wrote it after the game

was finished. In the time and space of the game, there wasn't room for reflection. There was only time to act. And so he acted.

Sam tossed the ball to Magic and cut through the lane. Josh set a pick to allow Sam safe passage. As Josh rolled off of that pick, Mike used the angles that were created to cut through and come open in the post. Magic tossed the ball inside. He did so with a smile on his face. And the pass sounded like a note from a flute as it traveled through time and space to land perfectly in Mike's hands. And the defense collapsed on Mike. So Mike passed the ball out to Nick behind the arc. Nick was open and he shot. The shot was like a perfectly formed smoke ring.

Woosh.

As the team traveled back to play defense, they were smiling and congratulating each other. It was magnificent.

"We were Magic Johnson," Sam later wrote, "so so were you."

Magic blinked again and the court vanished.

And music started to play. The basketball game bled into the song. There was a rhythm to *them* now.

At first, the sound was distant. It seemed to surround Sam and Nick. But then the sound started to gather momentum. And then the universe began to sing.

Sam caught the melody. He started to speak to Nick. His words sounded very much like the lyrics of the song *Wishlist* by Nick's favorite band, Pearl Jam.

"I wish I were a sacrifice," Sam's melody said, "but somehow still lived on."

Nick looked at Sam. Sam had given something of himself to get *there*. And both he and Nick were somehow living on, glowing as they traveled together.

And then Nick understood something. He started to speak. His words sounded very much like the lyrics from the song *Release Me* by Pearl Jam.

"I see the world," Nick's melody said, "feel the chill. Which way to go? Windowsill."

And as Nick's song spoke, *it* conjured his mother and his father. His adoptive, Midwestern parents as well as his Korean parents, the ones that he had never met. *They* were gathered together.

"Oh dear Dad," Nick's song said, "can you see me now? I am myself, like you somehow. I'll wait up in the dark, for you to speak to me. I'll open up, release me." Nick's words formed perfect rings of energy that drifted into the sky.

"I'll ride the wave, where it takes me," they said.

Magic nodded his head. He smiled. This was the rhythm he had been seeking. Here was the magic he had been trying to conjure.

Nick's voice bled into Sam's voice. So Sam picked up where Nick left off. It was good basketball now, so it would always be.

"I'll ride the wave," Sam echoed in time with Nick, "where it takes me."

Sam and Nick's words conjured their friends, their families. As they spoke, Sam's mom and dad appeared. Then his stepfather Jim was there as well as his wife Katie, his friends' Mike and Josh took clearer shape. Angus and Mary appeared. This song transformed all of them into all of *them*. Like mourners at a funeral or guests at a wedding, the ritual connected *them*.

And all of *them* would be okay because in that moment, in that space between spaces, all of *them* were *there*. So *they* always would be. After all, once something is conjured, it doesn't go away. *Their* energy ran wild.

In front of everybody, Sam looked Nick's mom in the eye.

"I'll hold the pain," Sam said.

Nick looked his mom in the eye. Then he looked to his dad. His music finished the line.

"Release me," Nick said.

And then Nick looked Sam in the eye. He smiled.

And then Nick's cigarette burned out. Nick

disappeared.

The universe, all of it as it has always been and always will *be*, reverberated with the conjuration of the sweet music of a connected human consciousness given permission to run wild. This was *traveling*. This was them becoming *them*. This was good basketball.

The harmony of this consciousness took shape as the final song on Pearl Jam's *Ten* album.

"Release me," it sang.

And it did. Release us, that is. All of *us. Always.*

We disappeared with a great big colossal woosh.

- CHAPTER 12 -

Of course the universe is far more complicated than our wants and needs. Need evidence? Go outside and look up into the sky. That shit is reckless.

To think that people get so caught up in their own comings and goings, their trials and tribulations, their specific versions of how things ought to be. They rage and rumble for brief and specific moments of time and then woosh, they transform. They can't help it.

Transform, did I say?

You cannot possibly imagine that we wink out, disappear. What a silly thought. Need more proof? Check out the complexity of what is going on inside of you. Something is being conjured *there*, something to fill the universe with. You can't shut that off with anything, not even a bullet.

Don't admit that in front of a judge though, they're liable to crucify you or something.

"What do you mean?" They'll ask. "Can't you be more specific?"

"No!"

Did I say crucifixion? I turn thirty-three next year.

That was pretty much it for Jesus. At least in that form. He transformed something fierce. You might've read about it. Europeans with firearms took that story everywhere with them over the past millennia or so.

That is how I showed up in America with a laptop at the turn of the 21st century. Me and my half-Jewish nose. We were a product of Scandinavian and Russian immigration, of western colonization. My father's Jesus-freakedness only made matters stranger.

So I haven't got much of a history. The history I do have is kept by way of my father's big, sarcastic mouth and my mother's dilapidated, alcohol-infused remembering.

Something tells me that my mom's mind somewhat resembles my writing. It rambles and oozes out from everywhere and nowhere at once.

I guess you work with what you've got.

At an early age I learned to take what adults gave with a grain of salt. Their gifts I would borrow, their faults I would let them keep. My mother's creativity stayed with me, her alcoholism did not. My father's charisma and sense of humor are here with me now. I have tried to leave his temper and anxiety behind. And I have done the same with the other people I've known who have taught me how to live.

Nick was one of those people.

I'd like to think that Nick's humor, intelligence, and sensitivity rubbed off on me. I'd like to think his rage, frustration, and stubbornness did not.

Jon Stewart was the host of the satirical *Daily Show* on Comedy Central. Nick couldn't get enough of Jon Stewart before he blew his brains out. Anyway, Stewart interviewed one of the people who taught me how to write, Kurt Vonnegut. I never met Vonnegut, but reading his writing freed me up to do what I have done here. Stewart got to speak with Vonnegut at the end of his life, before he transformed. He told Vonnegut this.

"As an adolescent, you made my life bearable."

Stewart had the chance to tell that to Vonnegut directly before he transformed. In front of a national audience, nonetheless! I was not so fortunate with Nick. So I'll say it here.

My friend Nick was one of the things that made my life bearable as an adolescent. Whether it was talking about the *Dune* books with him, playing *Madden Football,* or using our clever sarcasm to laugh our asses off about the people who made fun of us because I was short, pudgy, awkward, Jewish, whatever. Or because Nick was short, intelligent, sarcastic, Asian, whatever. We helped each other get through being thirteen.

Back then, he and I were like brothers.

And then I was an adult. And then Nick was dead. Time moved quickly, I guess.

Ten years after he put a bullet in his brain, my writing

helped me get through the complexity of him trying to end his life, of continuing to live on *there* instead of here. Did it help Nick? I'd like to think so.

Like Kurt Vonnegut had done for Jon Stewart, I tried to use my writing to create a vehicle to make my friend Nick's survival bearable. I created *them*. *They* were Magic, *they* were imagined versions of Nick and I, *they* were the universal song of people working together to play good basketball to survive.

As children, I loved Nick and he loved me. That love showed up in playing video games and in making jokes about each other. As I drifted into adulthood, I gave up some of what I had been in order to fit in at the University of Minnesota, with my girlfriend Julie, in school districts as a teacher, wherever.

Though we never talked about it, I think this bothered Nick. In talking with our mutual friend Tricia years after the suicide, I learned of Nick's journal that he kept in the months leading up to his suicide. On one page, he had made a chart. On one side of the chart were people who he felt were real. On the other page were people he felt were fake.

I wonder where I was on that list?

As I've already written, I never saw that journal. Nick's parents probably have it under lock and key. I don't think I'll ever see it. I don't think I need to. Let it go. Release it.

During his life, Nick never learned how to take what was good in people, leave their faults behind, and make peace with them. Had he learned that before his suicide, he might have seen that they were really *them*. That he was really *us*. Like it or not, we are all in this thing together. We are always shifting, shaping, and transforming, but we are also always connected.

Time taught me how to give into the endlessness of all of *us*, the *them* that transcends both time and space. Vonnegut wrote of this as our collective human consciousness in his final novel, *Timequake*.

159

By writing the first draft of this book, I taught Nick something of that lesson.

This happened in that impossible space. I am writing about dreams, the afterlife, or the imagination. Angus calls this the spirit world. My dad calls it heaven. Magic calls it *there*. When I was a child, my friend Jordan and I called it boogie land.

Whatever.

Prior to drafting the first version of this book, Nick often came to me in my dreams. These dreams were clouded and confused.

After drafting, Nick came to me less frequently. And when he did, things were clear and peaceful. They were intimate in a way they never were during our lives.

All of those dreams with Nick have always had a singular quality. They are real. *We* are *there*.

In fact, last night Nick appeared again.

Nick was in my car with my dad and I. I was driving.

Nick had agreed to go to lunch with my mom because I couldn't. By thirty-two, Mom was too much for me. There is another book in that statement. I am sorry, but I can't share her here much as I couldn't share Nick at the funeral for him ten years ago. Somehow, it seems important for time to move quickly to let that other story come.

Anyway, I was showing Nick where he would be taking my mom for lunch. Dad was reading my manuscript about Nick in the backseat.

I was proud of the ceremony I had conducted.

"I want the book to start like this," I told Dad in that dream, "ten years ago my best-friend Nick put a bullet in his brain."

And then I realized that Nick was sitting next to me. It was awkward.

"You know, because…" But I couldn't explain to Nick how I was writing a book about his suicide because he was so clearly alive.

160

Nick smiled. And all of the acrid, clever sarcasm was gone. He was peaceful. He took the manuscript from my father and started to read.

"It is okay, Sam," Nick told me.

Sure enough, when I woke up, everything was okay.

***

"Everything will always be okay, Baby, once we start living *there* instead of here." Magic's voice rang out one final time in my dreams, in my writing, in my consciousness. Then it was gone.

I wouldn't be seeing Magic again.

I was growing up.

***

This book transformed into a children's story about suicide.

It was a children's story because everything turned out *okay*. Even though Nick had put a bullet in his brain, it was possible for Magic to carry Sam to Nick, Nick to Sam, and both of them to a *place* where *they* could resolve Nick's shot with some good basketball.

The sequel to this book would be about Mom. It would need to be an adult's story because there was no resolution to the heaviness of her story. At least that is what I feel right now.

The third part of this trilogy will be about teaching. Teaching was the place where I took what I learned and I shared it with other people. This seems like redeemed innocence to me.

These books would be collections of stories about who I was, who I have been, and what I am becoming. And mostly they were about sharing me with you, turning us into *us*.

This place is Magic, baby.

Yes and I still won't pretend to be the smartest person that I know.

But writing this book did make me smarter.

One of the great things about *us* is how smart *we* can be.

But we have to be determined to survive in an enormous universe.

We can't give up. We can't put bullets in our brains.

***

"Nick still has something to say," Angus Poulin told me after I told him that I thought I was done with my book about Nick. "That is why he is still here in our conversation. There is a charge, Sam, something that has to be said."

Later, walking out of my friend and colleague's classroom, I realized that Angus was telling me to write the epilogue of this book, the thirteenth chapter, the end of this cycle. I was almost ready.

***

Nick came to me one final time last night. It was the first time since I finished forming this book about him.

I had been stressed out as of late. I was, after all, still a full time PhD student and a full-time English and Drama Teacher. And I was working on my dissertation about white identity now. That was another book entirely.

Being an adult is hard.

When I am busy, I seem more susceptible to dreams, to strange visions. So my mind was alive last night. You could say it was bursting with electricity.

Before I tell you about the dream, I want to tell you more about Angus.

Like I've written, the first time Angus saw a Hmong Shaman, his mother came to speak to him. She had recently passed away. After the first session, the Hmong Shaman told Angus that his mother was not transitioning from life to the afterlife well.

"There are many versions of the afterlife," the Hmong Shaman told him, "and some are not particularly pleasant."

During the second visit, Angus and the Hmong Shaman did some work to create more of a home for his mom in the spirit world. By the third visit, his mother was more at peace.

"It wasn't perfect," Angus told me later, "but she has a modicum of comfort now."

Angus told me that he would take me to the Hmong Shaman if I wanted to contact Nick. I told him I was going to write a book instead.

So I did. And the dreams about Nick went away.

Until last night.

Yes, and though he and I still knew that he had killed himself, something was different. He was happier. So so was I.

Instead of being in the blank space we usually inhabited in my dreams, we were in the upstairs of his parent's house. This is where we spent time before he moved deeper into his adolescent angst, his hatred of his mom and dad, and the basement of their townhome.

Nick was showing me a video he had made. Much like the German videos, he constructed a video where he had dubbed the commentary for a basketball game. Like Magic Johnson had commentated for the 2011-2012 NBA Finals, Nick created a satirical commentary for a college game. I laughed my ass off as Nick showed me this ridiculous footage of him commenting on a player taking the ball and bouncing it between his legs. The shot bounced off the back of the backboard and into the crowd.

"Such an unnecessary shot," he said.

I laughed and so did Nick.

Incidentally, that dream reminded me of one of the first things that Nick and I ever did together. We recorded a radio show on his parent's old boom box in sixth grade. Much as we had created comedy as children in that radio show and later as high school students in the German videos we had made, we were doing it again last night in my dream.

And after he showed me the video, he looked up and made eye contact with me. Nick never shared his feelings with me in reality or in my previous dreams.

"Sam," he said, "you are one of the only people who understands me."

In that dream, I pulled my head down because I didn't want Nick to see me cry. These would be the last tears I would shed for Nick.

And then I walked down the hallway to Nick's parent's bathroom. They were in the kitchen cooking dinner. Nick was helping. They were making us steaks.

Nick's parent's bathroom was completely remodeled. And there was a strange sort of tub next to the shower. It looked as though it were big enough for a baby.

Katie and I had been trying to have a baby for two years to no avail. But in the dream, it felt as though something was being born. Nick had something to do with it.

Yes, and this was the only dream that I had had about my friend Nick since I finished this book about him.

So I didn't visit a Hmong Shaman, Angus, but I did write this book.

And I wouldn't be seeing that version of Nick again, the one I knew while I was here.

Woosh, baby.

- PULLING THE +-
TRI+GGER

I came home after a long day of being a high school teacher and a doctoral student.

"How was your day?" Katie asked me.

"I am tired," I told her. I set my backpack on the floor. I dropped my laptop case on top of it.

"I have something that might cheer you up," she grabbed my hand.

Okay.

I followed Katie into the kitchen. She grabbed something off of the counter.

"Look at this," she was holding a pink thermometer.

"What is that?" I asked.

"Look."

It took me awhile to register the item. It had been a long day. I realized that she was holding a pregnancy test.

"Well?" She asked.

Katie and I had been trying for two years to get pregnant. I was convinced that it was a lost cause. Katie's cycle was irregular. My genetic history was a mess. I recently dropped off a sperm test at the doctor.

"It doesn't look good," the nurse had told me.

"Great," I had said.

So I was skeptical.

"I wanted to use my last pregnancy test before the appointment tomorrow," Katie smiled at me.

By the time she showed me the test, Katie had set up an appointment to see a fertility specialist at The University of Minnesota. I figured we were exhausting our options. So I was leery of the thermometer she was holding.

"Are you sure?" I asked her.

She was quiet.

"I just want to be careful," I told her, "with my history, I don't want to get too excited."

I knew it would be devastating to Katie if there were complications with the pregnancy. Everything around me seemed to contain complications. At thirty-two, I had learned how complicated and enormous the universe was.

It would be devastating for me if I couldn't help the baby inside of Katie survive in such a universe.

So I said a prayer. What else was I going to do?

Twelve weeks later, Katie and I were in a doctor's office. It was dark and the nurse was slathering slime on Katie's stomach. I sat silently as the image of our child took shape on the screen. A figure was squirming around inside of Katie's stomach.

"Baby is really moving around this morning," the nurse said.

She zoomed in on Baby's heart. It was furiously beating, determined to make a go of things.

I realized that I was crying as I listened to the child's heartbeat. I wiped at my eyes. There was such a long way to go yet.

As we left the office, I tripped over a chair.

"Are you okay?" the nurse asked.

"I am fine," I said.

***

I sat with Mary in her backyard.

"It is ready Sam, this book about Nick is finished. But I don't think the last chapter is right," she told me.

"The epilogue?" I asked.

"Yes."

I had written a thirteenth chapter. That seemed like the right number. It was the completion of a cycle, the age that Nick and I knew each other best, and the end of childhood.

The epilogue was a letter to Nick's mom and dad. In it, I thanked them for their parenting. I implored them to let go of their grief and guilt. I told them that this book was my attempt to transform the destruction of Nick's shot with an assault rifle into the healing love of a beautifully executed jumpshot.

I felt that I needed to justify to them why I had told this story. I offered it as my gift to them.

"That isn't the way to end this book, Sam. You should send them that letter, but this book isn't about them."

I paused. I thought about what Mary was saying.

It was a beautiful day in June. Another year as a teacher and a doctoral student had come to an end. I had just turned thirty-three. That morning, I had seen my child climbing around inside of Katie's stomach on an ultrasound.

By that time I had given myself permission to start telling my friends and my family that Katie was pregnant. I even told some of my colleagues and some of my students.

"You are going be a father? *You*?" They said to me.

I shrugged and gave them all a mischievous smile.

As I told Mary about the ultrasound, I confessed to her that the only person I had yet to tell about the baby was Mom.

"After Jim's suicide," I started to tell Mary that afternoon, "all Mom could say was the she wanted to die. She spent that whole day in a hospital bed, caked in her husband's blood, asking us to kill her, asking if she was dreaming. She tried to close her eyes so that she might wake up. I held her hand as she wept. I kept telling her that it would be okay, that I had survived suicide before, that she would be fine. But the only thing that seemed to ease her pain was when I asked her to stay alive so that she could meet her grandchild, I told her that Katie and I would get married and have a baby and that I wanted her around for that. She smiled and told me she would stay alive for that."

I paused. Mary listened intently. Her backyard was full of sunlight and birdsong.

"There is a heaviness to my mother," I told Mary, "that is what Katie describes it as. As much as I love her, I don't want that heaviness to transfer to my child. So even though Mom has now survived Jim by three years, against every diagnosis by every psychologist and doctor she has seen, I don't know if I am ready to expose my child to my mother."

Mary paused after listening carefully to me.

"That, Sam, is great material," Mary smiled at me.

My laughter filled her backyard.

On the way out of her house, I gave her a hug. And I continued traveling through this enormous, complicated universe.

I wasn't finished yet.

www.ingramcontent.com/pod-product-compliance
Lightning Source LLC
Chambersburg PA
CBHW020911180626
46816CB00007BA/2346